PRIME SUSPECTS

by

Geoff Collins

This book is a work of fiction. Names, characters, places and incidents are either the product of the author's imagination or are used fictitiously. Any resemblance to actual persons, living or dead, or to actual events or locales is entirely coincidental.

PRIME SUSPECTS

Copyright © 2020 Geoff Collins All rights reserved, including the right to reproduce this book, or portions thereof, in any form. No part of this text may be reproduced, transmitted, downloaded, decompiled, reverse engineered, or stored in or introduced into any information storage and retrieval system, in any form or by any means, whether electronic or mechanical without the express written permission of the author. The scanning, uploading, and distribution of this book via the Internet or via any other means without the permission of the author and publisher is illegal and punishable by law. Please purchase only authorized electronic editions and do not participate in or encourage electronic piracy of copyrighted materials.

The publisher does not have any control over and does not assume any responsibility for author or third-party websites or their content.

Front cover designed by Geoff Collins

Front cover art: Shutterstock File ID: 1372247075
Back cover art: Dreamstime File ID: 19323985
Interior art: Badge illustration Shutterstock File ID: 8613001
Interior art: Dog illustration: Pixabay CC0 Creative Commons Free for commercial use

Edited by Joe Gartrell and Ben Gibson of Word Mule. www.wordmule.com

Published by A&J Publishing, LLC
3266 Hartwell Street
Johns Island, SC 29455

Visit the author's website: www.booksbycollins.com

Categories: FICTION / Thrillers / Crime

ISBN: 978-1-951744-11-3 (eBook)
ISBN: 978-1-951744-12-0 (paperback)

Version 2020.03.24

www.projectpawsalive.org

A special thanks to Joe Gartrell and Ben Gibson of Word Mule.
www.wordmule.com

Nick Giordano Novels

"A Holy City Mystery Artfully Spun"

"Geoff Collins is a wonderfully versatile writer (check out his bibliography), and here, he weaves a delightful mystery set in the Holy City. Hop along and crack this case with Giordano—you won't regret, and it will get you primed for the other books coming along in the series."

"Well Written ... Interesting Characters and Plenty of Suspense"

"Good mystery with interesting characters and plenty of suspense. A cybersecurity expert is hired to determine if narcotics theft is taking place at Charleston SC hospital and who is behind it. Well written with lots of fascinating details."

"Wonderfully Crafted Story Set in Charleston"

"Wonderfully crafted story set in Charleston, SC—great story line and vivid imagery. Collins follows Giordano with insight and honesty. Can't wait for Nick's next adventure."

"A Fast and Exciting Read"

"The books are a fast read. Exciting and held my interest throughout. Hope to see more from this author."

"Another Wild Ride"

*"*Tools of the Trade *takes us on another wild ride with Nick Giordano and his crew. Collins, as he did with his previous book in this three-part series, deftly weaves on intricate story line that builds to a satisfying, thrilling end. Highly recommend Collins, a writer who deserves a vast readership."*

"Excitement and Suspense"

"Excitement and suspense as mafia and white supremacists fight over the drug market in Charleston SC. Characters well-developed and interesting story line."

"Hopefully More to Come"

"In this series, which sadly wraps here with Book Three, Collins found a higher gear with each, serving up a fresh batch of nasty folks for the series' core characters to root out and take down. That the books were set in Charleston only added to their delight. The only rotten aspect here is that this is the last we'll see of Nick Giordano and his pals—that is, unless, this crew comes around for cameos in one of Collins' future works. Hats off!"

Adam Stone Novels

Book 1

Book 2

Book 3

"The first thing we do, let's kill all the lawyers."
—**William Shakespeare**

PRIME SUSPECTS

CHAPTER 1

JOE WALLACE ALWAYS struck people as someone only a mother could love. Truth be told, Joe's mother wasn't all that fond of him either. He did, however, possess some impressive credentials: a law degree from Harvard, a clerkship with a prominent appellate judge, and an inside track to a partnership at the prestigious Charleston law firm of Jones, Sanders, and Cole. His success in the courtroom had garnered him a reputation as one of Charleston's premier defense attorneys.

More important than his legal prowess was his marriage to Elizabeth Buckley, the daughter of Noah Buckley, patriarch of one of the richest and most influential families in Charleston. Even in these modern times, there are only two ways to gain acceptance into traditional Charleston society:

birthright or marriage. After twenty years of marriage to Elizabeth, Wallace was not shy about taking advantage of the perks his place in the Buckley family afforded him. He also had developed a rather dubious reputation as a heavy drinker, gambler, and frequent user of various controlled substances—not to mention his notoriety for chasing skirts.

Wallace knew where most of the Buckley family secrets were buried—secrets that, if unearthed, would not only be embarrassing but also lead to serious legal consequences for the family. About fifteen years ago, Wallace had discovered that the pillar of the community, Noah Buckley, had in fact been involved in an insider trading scheme that netted the family several million dollars. And if that was not enough, the family had also for years been secretly donating to the American Freedom Party, an anti-Semitic, white nationalist organization.

Elizabeth was not blind to her husband's transgressions, but Wallace had made it crystal clear that he would drag her precious family through the mud should she ever try to divorce him. Not that he cared much about her as anything more than a rewards program that allowed him to pursue his vices while being the most expensively dressed person in the courtroom.

The Honorable Stephen A. Jackson of the Charleston County Circuit Court had just completed jury instructions in the murder trial of Alejandro Ruiz. Ruiz was a member of Charleston's East Side Posse and was on trial for the execution-style murder of Demarco Moore, a member of their rival gang, the Bloods. The gangs were in a seemingly endless battle for control of the Charleston drug trade. This was not the first time

Wallace had represented the Posse. His street source for cocaine, and on occasion heroin, just happened to be a member of the Posse. And it was made clear by the gang's shot-caller that unless Wallace agreed to handle some of their legal problems, information concerning his drug use just might find its way to the media. Not wanting to tarnish their pristine reputation, the partners at the firm allowed Wallace to represent the Posse as long as all proceeds were funneled through a separate company by the name of JAC Legal Assistance Inc.

Despite the overwhelming evidence clearly identifying Alejandro as the killer, Wallace's arguments created enough reasonable doubt to make a guilty verdict almost unthinkable.

Judge Jackson sent the jurors off to deliberate and then retired to his chambers. A moment later, the prosecutor approached Wallace and extended his hand. "You put on quite a show today, Joe," Thomas Smith said, "but we both know your boy Ruiz is guilty as sin."

Wallace ignored the expected handshake and replied, "It makes no difference to me whether his ass is guilty or innocent. He's going to walk, and we both know it."

Smith shook his head. "Christ, Wallace, you're a piece of work."

Joe just smiled and replied, "Here's a piece of advice from this piece of work, Tommy Boy: you might win more cases if you went back to chasing ambulances."

Wallace finished gathering his files, left the courtroom, and made the five-minute walk up Queen Street to Magnolias for a quick lunch. He ordered a Glenlivet single malt scotch and was scanning his messages when he saw one from his bookie, Derrick Lopez. Wallace preferred gambling on sports, especially when he'd been drinking, and a couple of recent bad moves had put him $50,000 in the hole. He normally wouldn't give this a second thought—Noah Buckley and Elizabeth always covered his gambling debt—but her asshole father was being a dick about covering it lately. It wasn't the first time Noah Buckley had done that, but Joe knew he could eventually persuade him to loosen the purse strings. The problem was that Derrick Lopez worked for Nick Santoro, who was connected to the Chicago mob, and they weren't exactly the most patient people.

Wallace knew he'd have to deal with Santoro and his debt, but for now he'd settle for the Glenlivet and his usual prime rib sandwich. He finished his meal and returned to his King Street office, where he relaxed and awaited notice that the Ruiz verdict was in. Another win would seal the deal on his partnership, which would also loosen up his father-in-law's wallet. He got the call at 3:00 p.m. and left for the courthouse. He was surprised the call came in so quickly.

The courtroom was almost full—a good portion being members of the East Side Posse and the Bloods. There was also a smattering of local reporters, prosecuting attorneys, and a few of Joe's colleagues from the firm. The tension in the courtroom was not as pronounced as you might expect in a murder case. Even the murder victim's fellow gang members seemed unusually resigned to the "not guilty" verdict.

Judge Jackson entered and instructed the bailiff to bring in the jury. As they filed in, Joe studied their faces for tells, but they were stoic, giving away nothing.

Once the jurors were seated, Judge Jackson began with the perfunctory thank-yous for their patience and attention during the trial. He then nodded to the foreperson and asked her to stand. "I understand you have reached a decision."

"Yes, Your Honor, we have."

The clerk retrieved the verdict notice, showed it to the judge, and returned it to the foreperson.

"Will the defendant please stand?" Ruiz and Wallace stood. The room held its breath as the judge nodded toward the foreperson. "You may read the verdict."

"On the first count, murder in the first degree, the jury finds the defendant, Alejandro Ruiz, guilty as charged." The foreperson went on to confirm guilty verdicts for the remaining three counts.

The judge nodded. "So say you all?"

"Yes, Your Honor," the jurors replied in unison.

"The court thanks you for your service. You are now free to go. Bailiff, you may remove the defendant." The judge banged his gavel. "Court is adjourned."

Wallace was stunned. There had to be some kind of mistake. Ruiz turned to him and said, "What the fuck?"

There was a commotion in the back of the courtroom, and Wallace looked behind him. The Posse's new shot-caller, Anthony "Spider" Gomez, was staring at him—his eyes burning with menace. He shook his head once and left the courtroom, followed by four of his underlings.

Ruiz was escorted from the courtroom, and Wallace slumped back into his chair, trying to process what had just happened. He was positive he had this one nailed.

"Hey, Joe. Did you hear that?" Thomas Smith queried.

Wallace turned toward the smirking prosecutor. "Hear what?"

"Sounds like an ambulance. Why don't you go chase it?"

CHAPTER 2

DETECTIVES ADAM STONE and Marcus Williams sat quietly in the back of the courtroom watching the spectators file out.

Marcus turned to Adam. "Well, brother, looks like our friend Alejandro is on his way up shit creek without a paddle."

Adam smiled. "Can't say that breaks my heart."

Both Stone and Wallace had put in more than twenty years on the Charleston Police Force, the last eight as partners in Captain Ed Merchant's elite Special Operations Division. The two detectives could not have looked more different. Marcus was 6' 4" and pushing 250 pounds. His chest and arms were huge. His neck seemed to be missing—his shaved ebony head merely an extension of his shoulders. Despite his massive size, it was his eyes that drew your attention. They were clear, cool, and profoundly intelligent.

In contrast, Adam was white, a few inches shy of 6', and a slender but solid 185. Their backgrounds were just as dissimilar. Adam was raised in the upper middle-class, predominately white Charleston suburb of Mount Pleasant, and Marcus grew up in the rough-and-tumble Union Heights section of North Charleston. But one thing they shared was an acuity for detective work. As a duo, they consistently led the department in closed cases.

Adam lived in a Johns Island apartment with his thirteen-year-old daughter, Piper. Piper attended Charleston Collegiate, a private school on the island where she excelled in the classroom and on the soccer field.

Almost two years ago, Adam's wife, Ann, was brutally murdered at the hands of what turned out to be a serial killer. In quick succession, three other women met the same fate, and for an agonizing year the investigation went nowhere. Finally, Adam and several other officers cornered and killed the murderer outside an abandoned church on Johns Island. Adam and Piper's lives were now slowly returning to some form of normalcy, even though the heartbreak and pain of Ann's loss would always be with them.

Perhaps one of the reasons the two detectives worked so well together was their love of sports. Marcus had been a middle linebacker and a four-year starter at Clemson University. He'd received second-team All-American honors his senior year. Despite his size, Adam had been a decent basketball point guard at Francis Marion University and continued to play in one of the highly competitive downtown Charleston leagues. Now in his forties, he'd lost a few steps but could still hold his own against the younger players. These games were a welcome respite from the pressure and stress of his job.

Adam and Marcus headed up a task force that investigated the ever-shifting landscape of players vying to control the distribution of heroin and cocaine in the city. They were at the center of a recent bust that upset the balance of power. The first victim in the resulting battle for dominance was Demarco Moore. He took a bullet to the back of his head from the Posse's Alejandro Ruiz.

Fentanyl-laced heroin, a potent concoction that led to a rash of overdoses and deaths, began showing up on the street about one year before. The shipments were coordinated by a Sinaloa Cartel lieutenant named Miguel Alvarez and sold on the Charleston streets by members of the East Side Posse. This led to an integrated effort between the task force, FBI, and DEA that resulted in the recovery of thirty kilos of product, $3 million in cash, and the arrest of Odell Davis, the shot-caller for the East Side Posse. The only disappointment in the operation was that Miguel Alvarez was never arrested. He escaped and made his way back to Mexico.

"There's already a shitload of bad blood between the Posse and the Bloods," Adam said. "The Ruiz verdict is bound to kick it up a few notches. Plus, did you see everybody playing it cool in the courtroom. We both know this shit's going to be settled on the street."

"Right. Ever since Odell Davis was sent away, Spider Gomez has been looking to make a name for himself."

"He's got a reputation of being a heartless prick," Adam added.

"Yeah," Marcus smiled and said, "but in his world being a heartless prick sometimes works surprisingly well."

Adam shook his head. "How the hell are we supposed to stay on top of all this shit?"

The courtroom was just about empty when Marcus checked his watch and said, "Let's take off. I just got a text from Merchant. He said one of Spider Gomez's bodyguards was just picked up on an outstanding warrant. Guy's name is Carlos Santana." Marcus smiled. "Yeah, Carlos Santana—just like the singer. They've got him down at Lockwood."

"I've heard of him," Adam acknowledged. "He's also Spider's main wheelman."

Adam and Marcus arrived at the Lockwood station and gathered more Santana intel from the desk sergeant.

"Big son of a bitch," the sergeant said. "Shaved head, tattoos, the whole nine yards. An officer pulled him over for running a stop sign and get this—he has an outstanding bench warrant for parking tickets! They got him down the hall in Room 1. Have fun, fellas."

"I'll give you the honors," Adam said and left for the observation room to watch Marcus interrogate Santana. Interview Room 1 and Room 2 were separated by a smaller room from which both could be observed and videotaped through one-way mirrors.

Santana sat at a metal table in the 10'x10' interview room. The room was stark—bright florescent lights, no window, no clock, no connection whatsoever to the outside world. The sergeant wasn't kidding about Santana's appearance. He was 5' 10" and looked like a bowling ball—if bowling balls were ever made from 250 pounds of tattooed muscle. He stared at Marcus but said nothing, trying to size him up.

"Mr. Santana, I'm Detective Williams." Marcus considered the clipboard he held. "Says here you've got $1,386 in outstanding parking tickets, and you missed your court date."

"This is bullshit," Santana said. "Parking tickets? Jesus Christ, just let me pay the suckers and get out of here."

Marcus glanced at his watch. "I'm afraid that's not going to happen, Carlos. It's after 6:00 p.m. on Friday, and there's no bail hearings over the weekend. Monday morning's going to be the earliest we can get you in front of a judge. You're probably going to spend the weekend at the Charleston County Detention Center. I can't promise anything, but work with me, and I'll see what I can do."

Santana was suspicious. "What the hell does that mean, and where's my car?"

"I'm sure your car's been towed to our Leeds Avenue impound lot. But like I said, answer a few questions and I'll see what I can do."

"What questions?"

"Word is you run with the Posse. That right, Carlos?"

"Yeah, I hang with them. So what?"

"Just wondering, that's all. Where do you work?"

"Nevin's Auto Repair. Fix cars."

"How's that working out for you?"

"Workin' out just fine."

"I take it you know Spider Gomez."

Santana paused and then set his gaze on Marcus. "Sure, I know him."

"Word on the street is Spider dropped a Code Red on the Bloods."

"I don't know shit about that, and if you think I'm going to give you anything so I don't have to spend the weekend in jail, you can just lock my ignorant ass up now!"

Marcus stood and walked toward the door. "Right. Just sit tight. I'll be right back."

As Marcus walked into the observation room, Adam asked, "So, what now?"

"Let's let Carlos cool his heels over the weekend."

"Right, that'll give us some time to take a look at his place," Adam suggested.

"No way are we getting a warrant."

"That's no reason we can't check it out. Listen, why don't I go in and shake him up. I say we put a tail on him when he's cut loose Monday morning. See what he does—where he goes and who he sees."

"Works for me," Marcus said.

Adam left for the interrogation room. He entered and got right to it—no introductions. "Hey Carlos, tell me something. Do you have to work at being an asshole, or is it just a genetic thing?"

"What you talkin' about?"

"Let's cut the bullshit. Who's supplying drugs to the Posse?"

"I don't know what you're talking about."

"Heroin. Cocaine. Who's supplying the Posse?"

"This is bullshit. Where's the other guy? I want to talk to him."

"Have a nice weekend, Carlos. Be nice to us, and we may just let you walk on Monday. Just remember this is us being nice to you when we don't have to. If we make a habit of it, your friends might wonder what you're doing for us." Adam left the room.

~~~

A despondent Joe Wallace left the courthouse and made the five-minute walk to his office. He had no doubt the Ruiz verdict had already hit the street and spread throughout the firm. He went directly to his office without so much as a nod to his secretary. "Hold my calls, Judy. I don't want to be disturbed."

He was about to close the door when she said, "Mr. Jones wants to see you in his office."

"Tell him I'm on a conference call, and I'll see him later." Wallace shut the door, tossed his briefcase on his Chesterfield leather couch, and headed directly for the bottle of Chivas in the bottom drawer of his Baroque walnut desk. He poured himself a healthy shot and downed it. *What the hell just happened?*
~~~

It had been more than a year since he'd lost a case, and that was only a third-rate embezzlement suit. He'd been untouchable when it came to murder cases. His eyes arced around his office. He felt right at home in the elegance—Brazilian Teak hardwood floors, Kashan oriental rugs, Paul Calle original paintings, mahogany paneled walls. *No one deserves this shit more than me.* He'd shifted his gaze to the stunning harbor view when his office door opened.

Without turning around he said, "Damn it, Judy. I said I didn't want to be disturbed!"

"How was your conference call, Joe?"

Wallace spun around on his heels and found Howard Jones and Matthew Cole standing at his door.

"Hope we're not interrupting," Jones said through a feigned smile. "But Matthew and I would like a few words."

"Of course." He nodded at the men. "Please have a seat."

They both remained standing. "This won't take long," Jones said. "We'd just like to know what happened today?"

"Hell, Howard. We knew Ruiz was guilty when we took the case."

"Excuse me, Joe," Cole said, "but I seem to remember you were the one who said it was 'a slam dunk.'"

"That's okay," Jones interjected. "As they say, 'can't win 'em all.'"

This helped Wallace relax for a moment, but his repose evaporated when Jones continued. "I seem to remember your little cocaine habit was the reason we found ourselves in bed with your Posse friends. And I also seem to remember we don't get paid unless you win the damn cases." He turned to Cole. "How much did we lose on this one?"

"Funny you should ask. I just checked. Looks like we're out of pocket about $20,000 and change."

All remnants of cordiality drained from Jones' face. "And don't forget you agreed to reimburse the firm if you lose one of your Posse cases. That won't be a problem, will it, Joe?"

"Of course not," Wallace said.

"Good," Cole said. Jones and Cole left the room without another word.

Joe remembered the look on Spider Gomez's face when the guilty verdict was announced. There'd definitely be blowback from Spider—he just didn't know what it would be. He'd deal with that later. Right now, he needed to come up with Derrick's $50,000 plus another twenty-grand for the firm—and he was flat broke.

"Judy, get my wife on the phone," he shouted.

He needed another drink, but before he could pour one from the Chivas that was still on his desk, Judy was at the door. "I'm sorry, Mr. Wallace, but your wife's out of the country. Your maid said she's on a cruise and won't be back until next Thursday. Do you want me to call Mr. Buckley?"

"No!"

He'd entirely forgotten about the cruise. But Noah Buckley was the last person Joe wanted to know he was in a financial shithole. He'd played the nice guy twenty years ago—coddling and cajoling Elizabeth until she finally agreed to marry him. But once he got his foot in the family door, it didn't take long before

Elizabeth's father began to despise him. A darkness fell over Joe that not even the glow of Chivas could penetrate. "Shut the damn door and leave me alone."

Judy Walker closed the door and smiled to herself. She'd worked for Joe Wallace for three years and thought he was a horse's ass. She was tired of covering for his drinking, gambling, and whoring. It was about time he finally got what he deserved.

Joe knew he was in trouble and didn't see any way to get out of it without Noah Buckley's help. His bank had made it clear that there'd be no more loans unless his father-in-law cosigned the note. In the past, Joe had even borrowed from the street knowing that Elizabeth would cover the debt and weekly vic. But that wouldn't work this time—Nick Santoro now controlled the city's loansharking racket. He needed to get out of the office and go somewhere to think.

~~~

Joe spent the bulk of his evening hours at The Harbour Club, a private spot overlooking downtown's Waterfront Park with a panoramic view of Charleston Bay. But when he was in the mood for some serious drinking and carousing, he'd head to Salty's on East Montague in North Charleston. It was still light when he pulled his Audi A7 into Salty's parking lot. He entered the bar, pausing a minute to allow his eyes to adjust to the dim surroundings. It was a Friday, but the place was dead. Two men were nursing beers and watching ESPN at the far end of the bar,
~~~

and an older couple sat in one of the six booths that lined the wall. Joe slipped off his suit coat, loosened his tie, and got down to some serious drinking.

The bartender nodded at him. "What can I get you, Joe?"

"Chivas on the rocks, Tony." He downed the scotch, the whiskey sliding across his tongue—followed by the warm and familiar burn. He returned the glass to the bar and pointed to it. Tony poured another.

As the evening wore on, Joe's confidence increased with each successive drink. *Spider's gonna be okay. He just needs a little time to cool off. And the firm needs me. I'm a damn rainmaker! I bet Howard would let the twenty-grand slide. Hell, I bet he might even front me money to pay off some of the fifty-grand I owe Santoro.*

By 9:00 p.m., Joe had a serious buzz on. He was feeling mellow, and his mood had definitely improved. He was watching the Hornets/Celtics game on TV when the door opened, and a couple entered. The guy was a big dude with a shaved head and arms covered with tatts. He wore a tight brown T-shirt and a pair of camouflaged hunting pants. It was clear Salty's wasn't the first bar the two had visited that night. The girl was tall and well put together, although she had a good number of miles on her. She wore skintight leggings and a cutoff T-shirt that left little to the imagination. They sat a few seats down from Joe and ordered two beers and two shots of Windsor. Joe stared at her for a while before his attention began shifting between her and the game. Eventually, he caught her eye, tipped his glass, and winked at her. He was somewhat surprised when she smiled back and blew him a kiss. She turned and said something to the guy she was with, and they both laughed.

By the end of the third quarter, Charlotte was up by two. Derrick Lopez had cut him off, but Wallace used one of his other bookies and dropped $500 on the Hornets. He'd figured they'd cover the twelve-point spread. But by the time the game was over, Boston had come back to trounce Charlotte by twenty. Joe was pissed. "Jesus, Tony, that's four in a row those bums have lost. Remind me to never bet on them again!" His attention swung back to the T-shirt woman. She was now by herself—the tatt guy must have gone to the head.

He called out to the bartender and pointed to the woman. His words were a bit slurred. "Hey, Tony, *gets* that lovely lady a drink. On me."

Tony pulled out a bottle of Bud from the cooler, opened it, and placed it in front of the woman. She gave Joe a seductive smile and mouthed, "Thank you, baby."

Joe stood, grabbed his drink, and made his way down to the bar to where the woman was seated. "You, my dear, are a beautiful lady. What's your name?"

"Bella." Her speech was also showing the effects of the shots and beers. "Thanks for the drink."

"You're very welcome, Bella. I was wondering …"—before he could say another word, he watched her eyes swing away from him toward the rear of the bar. He turned and saw her tattooed boyfriend leaving the restroom.

The smile left her face. "You need to go back to your seat, baby."

That was solid advice. However, Joe was full of liquid courage and pointed to Tattoo. "Tony, get that fella another beer. Put it on my tab." Tony took two steps to his right, reached under the bar, and took ahold of the handle of his sawed-off baseball bat.

Wallace raised his glass to Tattoo and said, "Hello there, my friend. Name's Joe Wallace."

The next thing Joe knew, his drink was flying across the room, and Tattoo had ahold of his shirt. "Take a hike, asshole!"

"Take it easy, man!" Joe said. "No harm, no foul. I got the message!"

Tattoo swung Joe around and pushed him against the wall. "Hey, Tony, tell Mr. Businessman to get the hell out of here before I lose my temper."

Still gripping the bat, Tony said, "Joe, you need to leave. Your tab is on the house."

"All right! All right!" Wallace said. "I'll leave. Just need to get my jacket. This place is a dive anyway."

Joe turned and took a few steps toward his seat. As soon as he passed Tattoo, he grabbed the bottle of Bud he'd bought for Bella, spun around, and smashed it across the side of the man's head. Glass, beer, and blood splattered across the bar and onto Bella.

Tony was over the bar in a second, bat in hand. He grabbed Joe's coat and threw it to him. "Get out. Get the hell out now!" Joe caught his coat and was out the door in a second.

Tattoo was sprawled on the floor, blood covering the side of his face. He was dazed but finally managed to grab the side of the bar and pull himself up. By this time, Tony was in front of him. "Let it go, Bobby! Not worth it. Let the son of a bitch go!"

Tattoo pushed Tony out of the way, burst through the door, and disappeared into the night.

CHAPTER 3

ADAM MET MARCUS at the station first thing Saturday morning. Adam checked out an unmarked Chevy Impala, and they left to take a look at Carlos Santana's place. It was a ramshackle brick bungalow with a detached garage tucked away on a cul-de-sac in North Charleston's Midland Park neighborhood. Four other houses were on the cul-de-sac—two of which were boarded up. Santana's lawn was overrun with tall grass and weeds, a fitting complement to the run-down house. The street was quiet, and nothing moved with the exception of a good-sized pit bull that stalked silently back and forth inside a chain link pen.

Adam pulled the Impala to the side of the road a few hundred feet from the house. "Let's leave the car here. We don't know if Santana lives alone. You stay here. I'll go knock on the door and if anyone answers, I'll come up with some story—I got lost looking for the Joneses or something like that."

Marcus laughed. "Yeah, partner. That makes sense. Some lily-white peckerhead comes knockin' on my door in the middle of this neighborhood? I doubt I'd be inclined to invite him in for lemonade. You stay put. I'll do it."

Marcus left the car, approached the house, and knocked. No one answered. He knocked again and waited a bit longer before peering through a front window. It was evident nobody was in the house, and he gave Adam the all-clear. They quickly walked around the house, checking each window as they went, and then moved on to the garage. The side door to the garage was locked.

"Be careful, partner," Marcus said. "Remember we don't have a warrant."

Adam smiled. "We're just gonna take a little peek."

After double checking that no one was around, Adam took out a small leather case and removed a tension tool and pick. He had the lock opened in less than a minute.

The garage was dark and smelled of motor oil, mildew, and neglect. Enough ambient light revealed a late-model Chevy Tahoe, its hood open, and several engine parts strewn on a wooden table next to a workbench.

"Our friend Carlos has a hobby," Adam said. "The Tahoe's obviously being chopped. We know the Posse operates a number of salvage yards in South Carolina, and our boy's doing his part."

"He told me he worked at Nevin's Auto Repair," Marcus said. "Looks like he takes his work home with him."

The pit bull began to bark, and Marcus whispered, "Not much more to see. Come on, we need to get out of here."

They were headed to the door when Adam held up his hand. "Hang on a second." An old metal desk was pushed against the far wall. Adam grabbed a rag and opened the center drawer. It contained a few auto repair manuals, as well as pens and pencils, a stapler, and assorted other office items—nothing of interest. He was about to close the drawer when he noticed a Bic lighter and a few small empty wax paper baggies behind the clutter in the back of the drawer. Three skulls were imprinted on each of the baggies. Adam found a blank no. 10 envelope in the drawer and carefully slid one of the baggies inside.

They left the garage and locked the door behind them, Adam using his shirt to wipe the lock and door handle.

"Can't say I'm surprised with what we found," Marcus said, as he slumped back into the Impala.

Adam shot a glance at him. "I looked inside the windshield—VIN plate had been removed. And take a look at this." He removed the envelope and handed it to Marcus. "Looks like Carlos has been chopping to support his chipping."

"Maybe so," Marcus replied, "but the problem is we broke into his garage, and there's that little thing called the Fourth Amendment—fruit of the poisonous tree and all that. We obviously can't use any of this to bust Santana, but he just might cooperate if he learns we know about his little chop shop."

"Maybe, but I wouldn't hold your breath. He knows what will happen to him if he plays show and tell. I say we let him know that we know about his side business and heroin habit and just keep an eye on him. Maybe he'll do something stupid. This is the first time we've seen these skulls on a heroin bag. We'll have forensics run a test on it. Hopefully they can chase down where it came from. Maybe the Posse has a new source for smack."

CHAPTER 4

ADAM AND MARCUS were back at the Lockwood station later that morning, and after dropping the skulled baggie off to the forensic techs, they left for the Leeds Avenue impound lot.

Adam parked the Chevy in front of the main office and walked around the building to a large holding lot that housed more than fifty cars and trucks. The vehicles were inside a ten-foot-tall cyclone fence topped off with razor wire. The small wooden shack just outside the main gate looked like a stiff wind would blow it over.

Tyrel Robinson had been a mainstay around the impound lot for the past fifteen years, and so was his old dog-eared South Carolina Gamecocks cap. He was relaxing inside his shack playing a blues riff on his harmonica with his feet propped up on a wooden crate when he saw the two detectives approaching. He reluctantly slid the jaw harp in his pocket and opened the door.

"Good morning, Tyrel," Adam said. "When are you going to get a new hat?"

"Don't need one. Which one you want today?"

"We're looking for a car that was brought in yesterday." Adam pulled out of copy of Santana's license plate number and handed it to Tyrel. "It's a 2015 red Dodge Challenger."

"Hang on." There was a large wooden board screwed to the wall just inside the door. Each key to the impounded vehicles had a yellow ticket attached, and Tyrel took a moment finding the key to the Dodge. He wrote the date and key number on a clipboard and had Adam sign it. "She's just inside the fence on the right. Come on."

Tyrel took his time walking to the gate—more of a shuffle than a walk. He pulled a chained set of keys from his pocket, unlocked the padlock, and gave Adam the keys to the Challenger. "Give these suckers back to me when you're done, and you gotta sign for anything you take out of the vehicle."

Adam smiled and said, "Whatever you say, boss."

"Don't be a smart-ass."

"Wouldn't think of it," Adam replied.

Adam and Marcus slipped on crime scene gloves and checked out the exterior of the car. They inspected the under-carriage, wheel wells, and grill work before using the key fob to unlock the doors. They spent another ten minutes going through the interior. The glove compartment held the registration and insurance card, the owner's manual, and a few receipts. A coffee cup, some lose change, and a few auto magazines were found—nothing suspect. Adam popped the hood and trunk.

"Take the trunk, Marcus. I'll do the engine."

A few minutes later, Marcus yelled, "Got something!"

Adam jogged to the back and saw that Marcus had removed the spare tire. He pointed to the base of the spare compartment. "Looks like a .38."

"I think we should leave it," Adam said. "If we remove it, Santana's going to know we searched his car."

"He'll probably assume we did that anyway. We'll leave it for now, but Merchant's got the final call on that."

"I know," Adam replied, "but I'm going to suggest we try for a warrant to attach a tracking device to the car. Remember Santana is Spider's driver."

Marcus was about to respond when his cell rang. He answered it and listened for less than a minute. "All right, Captain. We'll be there in fifteen minutes."

"What's up?"

"That was Merchant. A floater just washed up on the Ashley close to Higgins Pier. Ed wants us to handle it. Officers are already at the scene."

"Damn. Piper's having Chloe spend the night at the apartment tonight, and I was planning on taking them out to dinner."

"Change of plans, my friend." They headed to their car, tossing the keys to Tyrel as they left.

~~~
~~~

The Higgins Pier sat at the eastern end of the West Ashley Bikeway, and when Adam pulled up, a collection of fishermen and bikers was already pushing up against the crime tape and craning for a view.

Adam and Marcus lifted the tape and flashed their badges to the attending officer. "What do we have so far?"

"A 911 call came in about forty-five minutes ago," the officer replied. "The caller was fishing and said he saw what looked like a body on the shore about fifty yards upriver." The officer pointed to his left. "My partner's over there taking the guy's statement. The coroner and CSI will be here shortly. Come on, I'll show you."

It was low tide, and the body had come to rest in a patch of sweetgrass, waist up on the shore and the legs partly submerged in pluff mud. They were about twenty-five feet from the body when Marcus grabbed the officer's arm.

"Hold on! There's no way we tiptoe through that mud without screwing up the crime scene before our forensic techs get here."

From their vantage point, they could see a portion of the victim's head. Seaweed clung to the face, and it was clear that fish and land crabs had gotten to the eyes. It was definitely a man, and even from that distance, there was no doubt his throat had been sliced open.

The crime scene techs arrived a few minutes later and began assessing the area, taking pictures, and collecting evidence. One tech removed the man's wallet and placed it in an evidence bag.

Another tech made a notation identifying the manner, time, and place the wallet was removed.

"I didn't see any footprints in the mud," Adam said. "The body was almost certainly dumped and carried here by the tide."

Marcus was about to respond when they heard a voice from behind. "Looks like someone decided to take a swim."

It was Alice O'Sullivan, a Charleston County deputy coroner who had been around for as long as Adam could remember. She was in her mid-fifties, gray-haired, a bit portly. She wore a pair of baggy work pants, a black sweatshirt, and knee-high rubber boots. "What you got for me, detectives?"

Adam smiled. "It's a dead body, Alice."

"Oh, lovely! Let's have a look." She slipped on crime scene gloves and, after a nod from a tech, approached the body. "It's a fresh one. No evidence of bloating." She attempted to lift one of the man's arms. "Body is still in full rigor. Will someone give me a hand here?"

One of the techs helped Alice move the body onto land. She then removed a pocketknife, slit open the back of the victim's pants and inserted a rectal thermometer. After about thirty seconds, she removed it and check the results.

"At this point, the best I can tell is that he's been dead for between eight and sixteen hours. I may do better once I get him to the shop."

She then inspected the neck laceration. The left end of the cut started below the ear at the upper third of the neck and deepened, severing the left carotid artery and ending with a tail abrasion. "Not that I need to tell you, but we have ourselves a murder, gentlemen. Bag and tag him."

"When will you do the autopsy, Alice?" Marcus asked.

"In the next few hours. I should have preliminary information for you sometime tomorrow morning. But I can tell you that whoever did this sure as hell knew what they were doing."

Two techs were putting the corpse in a body bag when Marcus said, "Hold on!" He moved closer. "Holy Christ, Adam. Tell me I'm wrong, but that looks like Joe Wallace."

Adam leaned in. "Son of a bitch, I think you're right."

~~~

Adam and Marcus were in Ed Merchant's office back at Lockwood early that afternoon describing what they found at the pier.

"We're definitely going to be under the microscope on this one," Merchant said. "I contacted DA Stewart. She's on her way over."

"Marcus and I were at the courthouse Friday for the Ruiz trial. Shocked the hell out of everyone when the jury came back with a guilty verdict. Wallace put on quite a show, and we were convinced Ruiz was going to walk. Spider Gomez was there when the verdict came in." Adam smiled. "Spider was nice enough to flip the bird to us on his way out. Anyway, T.K. Carter and some of his crew from the Bloods were there too. We were surprised a fight didn't break out when the verdict was announced. After
~~~

shooting some visual bullets at Joe Wallace, Spider and his boys just quietly walked out of the courtroom."

"That's what I heard, too," Merchant said. The captain knew the murder of Joe Wallace and his relation to the Buckley family would make the investigation high-profile, and he wanted his best detectives on it. "Listen, I need you guys to shift from the drug task force and focus on the Wallace murder. Simmons and Covell will pick up your leads on your drug investigation. Brief me on the latest."

Adam brought Merchant up to speed on Carlos Santana and told him about the empty three-skull heroin baggie they found at his place. Merchant held up his hands. "Hold it right there. Where did you find that bag?"

"How about we found it on the street?" Marcus offered.

"Let's leave it at that," Merchant said. "Now what do you want to do with Santana?"

"We've got him at the detention center," Adam said. "He's already contacted a lawyer, so we figured he'd be cut loose Monday morning. We were planning on tailing him."

"I really think we might be on to something with Santana," Marcus added. "Word is he's really tight with Spider. He's not only his driver and bodyguard, he's also supposed to handle some of the Posse's wetwork."

Adam interrupted, "Listen, Ed, we were at the Leeds impound lot this morning casing Santana's car when you called Marcus. We found a .38 in the truck. We think we should try for a warrant to put a GPS tracker on his car. He's a good conduit to Spider Gomez. It's really important we keep tabs on him."

"I understand, and don't forget I know the history you two have with Gomez," Merchant said, as a hint of a smile appeared on his face. "I also seem to remember that the police officer's handbook discourages detectives from getting into fights with the suspect they're investigating."

Four or five months ago, Adam and Marcus ran into Spider and a few of his homeboys at Big John's Tavern in North Charleston. One thing led to another and words were exchanged. One of Spider's guys made the mistake of taking a swing at Marcus. The result was that two Posse boys spent the night in the hospital and both Marcus and Adam were suspended for a week without pay. Adam later admitted that the loss of the week's wages was worth every penny just to see Marcus in action.

"That's all good," Merchant continued, "but I told you I want you two on the Wallace case. Don't worry, I'll get Simmons and Covell on Santana. I doubt there's enough for a warrant, but I'll take up your idea of tracking Santana with them."

There was a knock, and then District Attorney Elaine Stewart stepped into the office. "Afternoon, Ed." She nodded at Adam and Marcus. "Detectives."

"Have a seat, Elaine," Merchant said. "Thanks for coming over. Detectives Stone and Williams will be prime on the Wallace murder investigation. Adam, tell Elaine what you know so far."

Adam again described the scene at the pier and the condition of the body. "O'Sullivan is starting the autopsy later today and should have something tomorrow morning. She initially estimated the time of death to be Friday night or early Saturday morning. We'll check the security cameras at Higgins Pier, but it's a public place and I'm sure the murderer would have known it would be monitored. Depending on the tide, we figure the body was carried to the pier after being dumped either upriver or downriver. CSI is analyzing the tide charts to see if they can get a rough idea of where. There's cameras on all the bridges crossing the Ashley. We'll have officers check them."

"Not to be disrespectful to the dead," Stewart began, "but Wallace was an ass. He was a hell of a defense attorney, but he was obnoxious, absolutely unbearable. He built up quite a reputation over the years and definitely had his share of enemies."

"Which brings us to suspects," Merchant said.

"There's certainly no shortage," Stewart said. "And the Bloods and the Posse have to be considered on that list. Ruiz took out one of the Bloods, and Wallace defended the killer. We know how that went down. Nobody's happy."

"Who else do you think might be on it?" Adam asked.

"Everyone in the legal community knows about Wallace," she said. "He's a big gambler, definitely has a drinking problem, can't keep his pecker in his pants. As you know, he's a regular Charleston aristocrat by way of marriage to Elizabeth Buckley, daughter of Noah Buckley. I know Noah, and he makes no bones about his feelings toward his son-in-law. He detests him. Wallace treats Elizabeth and the family like his personal ATM. I can't imagine why they hadn't kicked him to the curb long ago, unless Wallace had the kind of dirt on the family that smells as bad as his corpse."

"Okay," Merchant said, "I'll put word out to my people on the street. We'll see if they can pick up intel connecting the

Bloods or the Posse to the murder. It sounds like he was a heavy gambler. Detectives, I want you to find out the name of his bookie. Check out what kind of car he drove. If it's not at his house, it's got to be somewhere. Run a check on abandoned or towed vehicles. Also, I want you to see what you can get from Mr. and Mrs. Buckley and their daughter. You'll need to check out his law firm. Dig into his private life and focus on his movements after the trial. Where did he go from the courtroom? Who did he see? Let's get a timeline of his movements."

Merchant stood. "We're going to be under the microscope on this one. Mr. Wallace may have been an ass, but he was a high-profile one, and just because his peers hated him doesn't mean they're going to let us root around in their business. But it's still our job to find the son of a bitch who killed the son of a bitch."

Merchant shook Stewart's hand and walked her to the door. "Elaine, I'll keep you posted." Stewart left the room, and Merchant turned back to Adam and Marcus. "I'll have Gail get you the addresses for Noah Buckley and his daughter. Go ahead and notify the family. Get to work."

CHAPTER 5

THE MURDER OF Joe Wallace was fresh, and it was clear that Adam and Marcus would be working well into the night. Marcus let his wife, Makayla, know he would be at the station most of the night. Adam had already sent a text to Piper letting her know he wouldn't be able to take Chloe and her to dinner. He immediately called Tracy and explained he'd been assigned a new case and didn't know when he'd be able to make it home. It was far from the first time this had happened, and Tracy immediately agreed to spend the night at his apartment with the girls.

Joseph and Elizabeth Wallace lived in an upscale development on Daniel Island some fifteen miles from downtown Charleston. It was a favored choice for those with the means to escape the hustle and bustle of the city.

Adam rang the Wallaces' doorbell, and it was answered by a middle-aged woman dressed in traditional black-and-white maid attire.

"Good evening," Adam said. "Is Mrs. Wallace in?"

"No, sir."

"When do you expect her back?"

"She is traveling until later next week."

"I see," Adam said. "Do you have a number we can use to reach her?"

"No, sir. Mrs. Wallace does not wish to be disturbed while traveling."

Adam removed his detective shield. "Ma'am, it's important we contact Mrs. Wallace immediately. I'll need that number now."

The maid, face flushed, quickly gave Adam Elizabeth's cell number. She also told the detectives that Mrs. Wallace often puts her phone on "Do Not Disturb" while vacationing.

"Where is Mrs. Wallace?" Marcus asked.

"She's on a cruise to the Bahamas, but like I said, I don't believe you'll be able to contact her."

"We'll deal with that. Now, when did she leave on the trip?"

"That would have been a week ago Thursday morning," the maid answered.

"Thank you, ma'am." Marcus handed her one of his cards. "Please have Mrs. Wallace call us immediately should you hear from her."

Back in the car, Marcus dialed Elizabeth Wallace's number. It rang several times and went to voicemail. He hung up without leaving a message and pulled out the address for Noah Buckley. "Let's take a shot at the Buckleys. We can try Mrs. Wallace later."

The sun glistened off the blue waters of the Atlantic as they drove across the IOP Connector onto the Isle of Palms. Noah and Shelly Buckley lived in Wild Dunes at the far end of the island in a broad-shouldered house overlooking the lush and undulating 13th fairway. A row of windmill palms lined the driveway, and several sabal palm trees graced the manicured grounds around the house. Bronze statues of leaping dolphins flanked the main entrance. Marcus pressed the doorbell and a series of low chimes rang within the house. A moment later, a woman Adam assumed to be Mrs. Buckley opened the door. "May I help you?"

"Yes, ma'am. I'm Detective Stone, and this is my partner, Detective Williams. If you have a moment, we'd like to have a word with you and your husband. May we come in?"

Mrs. Buckley hesitated, then stepped back and pulled the door wide open. "Yes, certainly. What is this about?"

"If you could get your husband please."

"All right." She gestured to a large room that opened to the left off the foyer. "Please have a seat in the living room."

The room was expansive. Large oriental rugs covered the white Calacatta marble floor. The furniture was traditional, and the room looked staged—as if readied for a *Home and Garden* magazine photo shoot. Oversized seascape paintings adorned the walls. The house was elegant but somehow lacking warmth.

A few moments later, Mrs. Buckley returned trailing her husband. He was dressed in white slacks and a La Costa polo untucked at the waist. He was not a big man but carried himself in a manner that portrayed strength and authority—the type of individual who commands a room without saying a word. "What can I do for you, detectives?"

Marcus introduced Adam and himself and nodded toward one of the sofas. "You may want to have a seat, sir."

Mr. and Mrs. Buckley sat, both looking as though they were prepared to hear the worst.

Marcus nodded to Adam, who delivered the news. "We're sorry, but we need to inform you that your son-in-law, Joseph Wallace, has been found dead."

Mrs. Buckley sucked in air, a sibilant intake. Mr. Buckley didn't flinch, but simply asked, "What happened?" Adam briefly explained where the body was found—leaving out the gruesome details. "I assume there was foul play," Mr. Buckley said without emotion.

"Yes, sir," Adam responded. "I'm afraid there was. We stopped by your daughter's house and were informed she left on a trip over a week ago. We've tried her cellphone but haven't been able to get in touch with her."

Mrs. Buckley sat quietly—her gaze focused in the middle distance.

"My daughter is on a cruise to Nassau with some friends of hers," Mr. Buckley finally offered. "She mentioned they planned to charter a yacht and visit some of the outer islands. I'll try to get ahold of her and arrange for her to fly back home. I'm sure you'll want to speak to her."

"Yes, sir, just as soon as possible," Adam said. "Did she happen to mention the name of the charter business that was used?"

"I believe it was a company called Stan's and Sam's Boats or something like that." Marcus wrote down the name.

"I realize this is a shock to both of you," Adam continued, "but we'd like you to answer a few questions."

Buckley turned to his wife. "Shelly, dear. Would you please make some coffee for the detectives?"

"Certainly." Mrs. Buckley touched her husband's shoulder as she left the room.

Adam was intrigued by the couple's non-reaction. He didn't expect them to break down and wail—he knew there was no love lost between the Buckleys and their son-in-law—but still, Adam found their stoicism strange.

Once she was gone, Mr. Buckley leaned toward the detectives. "Who killed him?"

"At this point, we don't know, sir. We're just beginning our investigation. Did your son-in-law have enemies, anyone who might have had reason to do this?"

"Enemies?" Buckley said, a faint smile evident. "How much time do you have, Detective Stone?"

"Excuse me, sir?"

"It's no secret Joe had enemies. Plenty of them. You may have ascertained that we were not all that pleased with Joe. He was an embarrassment and a liability to our family. There's no doubt he was an effective defense attorney, but that's where it ended. In every other respect, he was a weak man."

Mrs. Buckley returned with a tray of coffee.

"Mr. Buckley," Marcus said, "can you think of a specific person or group who may have wanted to do him harm?"

"Well, Joe was often in debt to some unsavory characters. Gambling—it controlled his life. We'd always taken care of these debts, but they'd increased lately and become more frequent. When he didn't pay, they threatened him—Elizabeth too. In addition to his drinking, he used cocaine on a fairly regular basis, and I'm sure that led to more trouble. You asked if I could think of a specific person or group that might have done this. The answer is no—no one specific. But I'm sure they're out there. Gentlemen, it may sound harsh, but I can't say we're broken-hearted over the news of Joe's death."

The tray of coffee was left untouched.

An uncomfortable silence fell over the room until Shelly Buckley stood. "I think I'll excuse myself." She turned to her husband. "I'm going to lay down, dear. Could you please show the officers out?" She nodded to the detectives and left the room.

Once she was gone, Mr. Buckley gestured toward the front door. "I'll walk you out."

"Thank you for your time, sir," Marcus said. "I'm sure this is a difficult time for you and your family."

"I appreciate that, detective, but I'm sure we can deal with it." A hint of a smile flashed across his face.

Adam and Marcus gave Mr. Buckley their cards. "Please let us know as soon as you make arrangements for your daughter's return," Adam said. "It's critical we speak with her as soon as possible. And I'm sure we'll also want to talk with you and your wife again."

"Of course. I'll have Elizabeth back home as soon as possible. Now, detectives, I believe this is where you ask me where my wife and I were Friday night. Correct?" Adam and Marcus remained quiet. "Shelly and I were at our next-door neighbors, Frank and Mary Richardson. We returned here around 10:00 p.m. that evening and spent the rest of the night at home. You're more than welcome to confirm that with the Richardsons."

"Yes, sir, we will," Adam said. "Again, please contact us as soon as your daughter returns. Mr. Wallace's body is with the coroner. I'm sure she will contact you regarding when you and Mrs. Wallace can claim the body. And let us know if you think of anything else that might help us find the person or persons who did this."

Adam was backing out of the driveway when Marcus glanced behind him. The silhouettes of Shelly and Noah Buckley were standing at the front door arm in arm.

~~~

"Well, that was weird," Marcus said. "I got the feeling Buckley wanted to break out the champagne and make a toast!"

"That's probably what they're doing right now," Adam said. "I don't know whether you caught it when Buckley gave their Friday night whereabouts."

"Yeah, what about it?"
~~~

Adam smiled. "We never said Wallace was killed on Friday."

"I didn't catch that, but you're right. Logical assumption, though?"

"Maybe," Adam said. "We'll follow up with their neighbor tomorrow, but Noah Buckley is definitely on the board. Wallace treated his daughter like shit. Plus, Elaine Stewart told us she thought Wallace might have dirt on Buckley and his family. That's a hell of a motive if you ask me."

Marcus nodded.

"Did you notice Noah Buckley only referred to Wallace in the past tense—almost like he already knew he was dead?" Adam asked. "He also said Wallace's gambling was catching up with him. We know Nick Santoro runs the gambling, numbers, and loansharking racket in Charleston, and he's hooked up with Chicago. Those guys don't screw around. Plus, we know Wallace liked his nose candy, and that stuff's not cheap. The dude had expensive habits. Where's he getting all his money?"

"Everyone says he was a heck of an attorney, and he must make some decent coin," Marcus said. "And we know the Buckleys have deep pockets. But with all his bad habits, it doesn't surprise me he might be broke most of the time."

"Okay," Adam said. "Let's back up and see where we are. Who'd want to see Wallace disappear? We can start with the Bloods and the Posse. Number one: Ruiz offed the Bloods' Demarco Moore … Wallace defends Ruiz … Bloods are pissed. Number two: Wallace defended Ruiz … Ruiz was found guilty … Spider and his Posse are pissed. Number three: Wallace can't pay his gambling debts … Santoro and Chicago are pissed.

Number four: Wallace might not be able to cover his drug debt … dealer is pissed. Number five: Wallace had dirt on the Buckleys … Wallace is dead … dirt disappears."

"Christ, Adam. It's getting crowded."

"Yeah, and I get the feeling there's more to come."

As soon as they got back to the station, Adam googled charter boat companies in Nassau and the Bahamas with variations of the name Sam's Boats. After striking out a few times, he was able to find an outfit named SamBoat.com. His call was answered by the owner's wife. He explained who he was and the situation concerning Elizabeth Wallace. After giving her both Noah Buckley's and his own cellphone number, she assured Adam the information would be given to her husband.

It had been a hectic few days, and Adam and Marcus began the process of organizing the investigation and setting priorities. An integral part of any murder investigation is the creation of what's called the murder book. In law enforcement terminology, the murder book is the complete case file of a murder investigation. It typically includes crime scene photos and sketches, autopsy results, forensic reports, and transcripts of investigator's notes and witness interviews. The murder book creates a paper trail of the investigation—from the time it is first reported until the suspect is arrested and charged.

It was approaching midnight. They would be spending the night at the station and decided to take turns catching some sleep—Adam taking the first shift and Marcus heading to a room on the second floor known as the Bunkhouse.

Adam woke Marcus at 3:00 a.m. and caught a few hours himself before making a quick trip home to shower and check on Piper and Tracy.

CHAPTER 6

ADAM GOT TO the apartment by 5:30 a.m. Sunday morning. He had no doubt Piper and Chloe had stayed up most of the night doing whatever it is teenage girls do. Adam knew there was no way they'd wake up until much later that morning.

He was at the kitchen table writing a note to Tracy when she walked in. "Good morning," he said. "Sorry, but I've got to get back to the station, and I'm not sure when I'll be back home." He pulled out his wallet and put $50 on the counter. "Maybe you could take the girls to Tattooed Moose for Sunday brunch. I feel bad about messing up our dinner plans last night."

"Not to worry, dear. You do what you need to do, and we'll be here when you get back. You go on now."

"Thanks, Tracy. You're the best."

~~~

Marcus was at his desk in the bullpen when Adam returned. Just as Adam moved to sit down, his phone rang. He answered it, covered the mouth of the phone, and told Marcus it was Alice O'Sullivan.

"Alice, what have you got?" He removed his pen and notepad and took notes for the duration of the brief call. He hung up and said, "Alice is still waiting on some lab results, but she wanted to give us her initial findings. Most is what we expected. Wallace had traces of alcohol and cocaine in his system and was obviously dead before he was put in the river. Some of the flesh around the neck incision was torn, indicating the knife had a serrated blade—more likely a hunting knife than a switchblade. No evidence of defensive wounds, which makes me think Wallace was either completely surprised by the killer or knew him. And it looks like he was tasered. She found two holes in his shirt and puncture marks on his chest. But here's the most interesting thing: a $100 bill was stuffed halfway down his throat."

"What's up with that?" Marcus asked.

"I don't know. Got to be some sort of message. It sounds like something the cartel or a mafia hitman would do. The lab's got it now, but I can't see how they'll get anything off it."

"It obviously means something," Marcus said. "Could have been done by the Posse for Wallace losing the Ruiz case. And you got to figure he also probably owed them money for the drugs he bought."
~~~

"Maybe, but why kill him if he still owed them all that money?" Adam offered. "Sure, he lost the case, but I can't see them killing him for that."

"My gut says it's Santoro and the Chicago mob making an example of what happens when you don't pay what you owe them," Marcus explained. "And it's not out of the realm of possibility that Noah Buckley might have hired someone to kill him. Did O'Sullivan find anything else?"

"Yeah," Adam replied. "Looks like cocaine wasn't the only drug Wallace was into. There was a baggie with three skulls in his pants pocket, just like the one we found at Santana's. We know he got his drugs from the Posse, and that helps to confirm they're probably working with the cartel."

"Right, but that doesn't help us figure out who killed Wallace," Marcus said. "Maybe we'll get something from the lab results. But there won't be much physical evidence, not after the body spent all that time in the water."

~~~

A few minutes later, Adam took a call from Ed Merchant. He was told that one of Merchant's undercover detectives, Terry Blackwood, had come up with some street intel on the Posse and the Bloods. He gave Adam a phone number to call Blackwood. Adam grabbed a piece of paper and wrote it down. After hanging up the phone, Adam held up the piece of paper. "Terry Blackwood's got some information for us, and Merchant gave me a burner phone number to get ahold of him."
~~~

Terry Blackwood had spent the last six years as an undercover vice detective working the seedy underbelly of Charleston's drug scene. Adam and Marcus had worked with him on several drug investigations over their years as part of Merchant's Special Operations Division. Terry played the part of a low-life street addict to perfection and, by doing so, had ingratiated himself with several street pushers and members of both the Posse and the Bloods.

Adam called the number, and Blackwood answered with a simple "Yeah?"

"Terry, it's Adam Stone." Adam was about to tell him about the note, but Blackwood interrupted.

"I'll meet you in the Citadel Mall parking lot across from Dillard's." The line went dead. He hung up the phone and repeated Blackwood's message to meet at the mall.

Being early Sunday morning, traffic was almost nonexistent and the Citadel Mall parking lot deserted. Adam pulled his Charger into the mall lot and noticed an old beat-up Chevy Cavalier parked at the far end across from Dillard's. A man was leaning against the passenger side door. When he got closer, he recognized Terry Blackwood. Adam drove up alongside the Chevy, and Blackwood slid in the back seat of the Charger. "Drive," was all he said.

Blackwood had long blond hair tied in a ponytail and wore a pair of old jeans and a loose-fitting Hawaiian shirt. There was a thick leather necklace hanging around his neck. His eyes were bloodshot, and he was alarmingly thin; his anemic face looked like it hadn't been shaved in a week or so.

"It's been a while, Terry," Adam said. "How've you been?"

"Livin' the dream, boys. How's the civilized world?"

"Not so civilized lately," Marcus said.

"Yeah, I heard that Wallace lawyer got wasted, and you guys are point on the investigation. Merchant got in touch and wanted information on how the street's taking the news."

"And what's the word?" asked Adam.

"Word on the street is Wallace was into his bookie for a good piece of change, and he'd run out of get-out-of-jail-free cards. There was even rumblings that Chicago was considering making an example of him. He got his drugs from the Posse, and he was underwater with them too. Spider Gomez thinks Wallace screwed up Alejandro Ruiz's murder defense. He's not a happy camper. All in all, Wallace had an affinity for pissing people off. Looks like it finally caught up with him. Nobody knows who took him out, but nobody was surprised or sad it happened."

"That's what we heard," Adam said. "Here's something else. The coroner was doing the autopsy on Wallace and found a $100 bill stuffed down his throat. What do you think?"

"You two should know it's not unusual to find something put in the mouth of a murder victim. Rapists are sometimes found with their private parts stuffed in their mouth. Bags of heroin or meth have been found in the mouths of murdered drug dealers. And I've heard of a few professional hitmen that would do it if the killing had to do with money. Somebody's sending a message, and it could really mean a payback for almost anything."

"Any information about the Bloods coming after the Posse for killing Demarco?" Marcus asked.

"Obviously, it depends who you talk to, but here's the skinny. There's no doubt Ruiz took out Demarco Moore, and street justice dictates the Bloods will go after someone in the Posse. It's an 'eye for an eye' world out there. But Ruiz was found guilty and is going away for a long time. There's a chance the killings might be finished for the time being. But there's always the chance someone will go rogue and the whole thing will start over."

"Right," Marcus said. "Let's just hope cooler heads prevail."

"That may be wishful thinking, but we'll see. Either way, you two are fair game—especially for the Posse. You took down Odell Davis and busted up their lucrative drug alliance with the cartel. Spider's the new kid on the block and needs to cement his rep. I wouldn't be surprised if he takes a shot at you two. I think he'd be stupid to do that because of the blowback the Posse would get from the department. Anyway, just watch your back."

"We know that," Adam said. "Merchant put us on the Wallace case, but what can you tell us about who's making a move to control the drug trade? We came across some heroin with three skulls printed on the baggies. Have you heard anything about that?"

"Yeah, word is that the Posse's back in bed with the Sinaloa Cartel. I've seen the three-skulled shit on the street, but it's only been around for a few weeks. I figure the cartel is testing how it sells and how well the Posse moves the product. This new stuff is supposed to be laced with a small amount of fentanyl, and it's got a real kick to it."

"What about the Bloods?" Marcus asked. "Are they still in the mix?"

"Maybe, but my gut tells me not so much anymore. The Bloods have lost a lot of street cred over the last year or two. The only problem is that their shot-caller, T.K. Carter, might do something rash to get them back."

"So, you're saying the Posse is more of a suspect in Wallace's murder than the Bloods," Adam said.

"Right. Although, to be honest, I can't see how it made sense for either to take a run at Wallace. They've got enough problems with each other. Neither wants more attention from the cops than they're already getting."

"Yeah, that makes sense," Adam said. "Any word on how the cartel is bringing in the skulled product?"

"No, not at all. Like I said, I think the cartel is still testing the product and how well the Posse distributes it before they bring in a major amount of it."

"Thanks for the information, Terry. Just let us know if you learn anything else about the Wallace murder or the three-skulled heroin."

"You got it," Blackwood replied. "Now take me back to my ride. The last thing I need is to be seen with you two yahoos."

~~~
~~~

They had yet to confirm Buckley's explanation that they had spent most of Friday night at their neighbors' house and made the drive to Isle of Palms to interview the Richardsons.

The Richardsons' house was somewhat smaller than the Buckleys' but definitely a showcase home in its own right. A pleasant-looking woman Adam gauged to be in her early fifties answered the door.

"Mrs. Richardson?" Adam asked.

"Yes."

Adam introduced himself and Marcus and explained they had met with Noah and Shelly Buckley the day before and had a few questions for her and her husband.

"Dear Lord, this is about poor Joe Wallace, isn't it?"

"Yes, ma'am. May we come in?"

"Certainly." She led the detectives into her living room. "Owen, that's my husband, is playing golf today. How can I help?"

"Thank you, ma'am," Adam began. "The Buckleys told us they had spent Friday evening at your house. Do you happen to remember what time they left?"

"Oh, dear. Let me think. I would say they left shortly after we finished dinner. Around 8:30 p.m., I believe. Poor Shelly was feeling under the weather. I hope she's doing better."

"I see. Have you met their son-in-law, Joseph Wallace?"

"Yes, once or twice," she replied. "Seemed like a nice young man. He didn't come by very often, I guess."

Adam stood and said, "We're sorry to interrupt your day, Mrs. Richardson. You've been very helpful."

"I hope Noah and Shelly can get through this. So sad."

"I'm sure they'll manage and thanks again." Adam and Marcus left and went directly next door.

Noah Buckley answered the door. "Detectives. Back so soon?"

"Just a few more questions, sir." Adam said.

"Of course. Come in."

After taking seats in the living room, Adam began. "We'd like to clear something up. We just spoke to Mrs. Richardson, and she indicated that you and Mrs. Buckley left their house about 8:30 p.m. Friday evening. She said your wife wasn't feeling well."

"Yes, that sounds about right. Stomach bug or something."

"I see. We seem to remember you saying you got back to your house at 10:00 p.m. that night."

Buckley paused for a moment before answering. "Yes, that's correct. Shelly wanted some fresh air, and we took a walk on the beach."

Adam waited for a further explanation but got none. After an awkward pause, he asked if he'd been able to get ahold of his daughter.

"Yes, she actually called me late last night. I understand you were able to talk to the chartering company, and they located her Elizabeth and her friends were on one of the outer islands. The captain's returning to Nassau, and I was able to get her on the last flight out Tuesday night. She's scheduled to arrive in Charleston sometime after midnight early Wednesday morning."

"How did she take the news of her husband's death?" Marcus asked.

"I'm sure she was devastated, detective." His voice was tinged with a hint of sarcasm.

"Well, it's good to know she'll be back Tuesday night," Adam added. "We'll plan to call her first thing Wednesday morning. Thanks again, sir, and you have a nice day."

~~~

Adam pulled out of the driveway and commented, "Hell of a long walk."

Marcus shook his head and with a good bit of cynicism said, "You think so?"

"Listen, we both know there's no way Noah Buckley is going to slit anyone's throat," Adam said, "but I'm not ready to discount the possibility that he might have hired someone to do it."

"Perhaps. I remember Terry said Derrick Lopez was Wallace's main bookie. I say we take a run at him and see what we learn."

Derrick Lopez had been making book in Charleston for more than a decade. He moved around but, for the most part, worked out of a bar at the corner of Spruill and Calvert in North Charleston called Gino's. It was a small wooden building well past its prime—its weathered metal door and iron-barred windows both bled rust. Gino's opened in the early '70s and hadn't changed much since then.
~~~

Adam parked in front of the bar, and they entered through the heavy metal door. The inside smelled of cigarette smoke and stale beer. A ten-seat bar ran along the left wall. There were a few tables, a jukebox, and a single pool table in the back dimly lit by a hanging light. Both Adam and Marcus had been there a few times before and nodded at the bartender, who looked like he'd been tending ever since the place opened. As soon as their eyes adjusted to the dim interior, they spotted Derrick sitting near the end of the bar reading *Sports Illustrated* and nursing a Bud Lite.

Adam took a seat to his right and Marcus one to his left. "Hi there, Derrick," Adam said. "How's business these days?"

"Same old, same old. You gentlemen care to place a wager? The Nicks and Nets are even money tonight."

"Maybe some other time," Adam answered. "What can you tell us about Joe Wallace?"

"Don't believe I know the man." Marcus put his hand on the back of Derrick's neck and squeezed. "All right, all right! Christ let go. I know him."

Marcus removed his hand and gave Derrick a pat on his back. "That's better, now talk to us."

"Listen, I know he got whacked. I had nothing to do with that."

"We heard Wallace was into you for some serious money. How much did he owe?"

"Enough."

"Enough as in how much?" Marcus pushed.

"Almost fifty big ones," Derrick said. "He'd always been good for it. Whenever it got a little out of hand, his father-in-law would ante up."

"And that didn't happen this time?" Marcus asked.

"Don't know. I was just told to stop taking any more of his action."

"How long ago was he cut off?"

"I don't remember. Maybe three or four weeks."

"So what happen to the fifty-grand debt?" Adam asked.

"Not my worry anymore."

"Derrick," Adam said, "we know you work for Nick Santoro. What did he do about the fifty-grand?"

"I don't know. That's way above my pay grade. And like I said, I had nothing to do with anything."

They figured they'd get nothing more from Derrick and stood up to leave. As they were walking out, Adam turned back and said, "Hey, Derrick. You want a piece of advice?"

Derrick look concerned. "What?"

"No way are the Nicks beating the Nets tonight."

~~~

Back at Lockwood, they had just sat down when Merchant waved them over to his office. "Did you see Blackwood?"

Adam updated the captain on their meeting with Terry, as well as O'Sullivan's autopsy update, the follow-up with the Richardsons and, finally, their meeting with Derrick Lopez at Gino's.
~~~

"What about the wife, Elizabeth Wallace? Have you found her?"

"We have. She was on a yacht vacationing in the Bahamas for the past ten days or so. She'll be flying out late Tuesday night, and we plan to interview her first thing Wednesday morning."

"Good. By the way, I left both of you a message. I've arranged for you to meet Howard Jones, the managing partner of Jones, Sanders, and Cole, at 9:00 a.m. tomorrow morning at their law firm's downtown offices."

It was after midnight when Adam finally began to construct a timeline of the Wallace murder and its suspects. They had commandeered one of the small conference rooms in which to work and store items connected to the case. There was a long whiteboard on the far wall. Adam made two entries. At the top left-hand side of the board, he wrote:

Friday: 4:30 p.m.—Guilty verdict, Ruiz case

At the bottom far right of the board, he wrote:

Saturday: 12:30 p.m.—Wallace body found at Higgins Pier

As evidence was collected and information discovered, dates, times, and descriptions would be added to the board—creating a visual timeline of the crime.

CHAPTER 7

ADAM AND MARCUS were back in Captain Merchant's office first thing Monday morning. Despite a chronic lack of sleep, the detectives were acutely aware that it had been more than two days since Wallace's murder. They were anxious but committed to do what was necessary to move the investigation forward.

"While you're at the law office, talk to Wallace's secretary, assistants, everyone who worked with him on a daily basis," Merchant instructed. "You know the drill. Now, what about warrants for phone and bank records for Joe Wallace?"

"We'll get those to Judge Roberts today," Adam replied. "We're also going to request ones for the Buckleys and Elizabeth Wallace."

Jones, Sanders, and Cole occupied two floors in the Halston office building on King Street. Marcus and Adam arrived a little ahead of schedule and sat in one of several Bernhardt leather chairs—each no doubt costing thousands. Paintings of past partners hung on dark mahogany walls—a bit of smugness captured in all their demeanors. Eventually, a tall woman who looked like she came straight out of a *Cosmopolitan* advertisement led them to Jones' office.

He was on his feet and waiting for them when they walked in. "Gentlemen, please come in and have a seat. May I get you coffee or juice? A muffin or croissant perhaps?" They both declined. "All right then. I told Mr. Merchant we'd do whatever we can to help find out what happened to Joe. That being said, this could potentially be quite embarrassing for the firm, and we'd appreciate if you could limit our public exposure. Much of Joe's work was carried out through a separate company called JAC Legal Assistance. If you have to identify the company, please use that name."

It was immediately clear that Jones was more concerned with minimizing the potential impact on the firm than seeking justice for the death of one of his associates. They'd yet to find anyone who seemed to give a shit about Wallace.

"Thank you for seeing us, Mr. Jones," Marcus began. "We know Mr. Wallace lost the Ruiz murder case last Friday. I'm assuming you saw him after the trial. What can you tell us about his state of mind after receiving the verdict?"

"Joe was an excellent defense attorney and rarely lost a case. He was obviously disappointed." Marcus waited for Jones to elaborate, but he simply smiled and sat there silently, letting a little awkwardness build.

After a moment, Adam moved on. "Do you know what time he left the office that night?"

"I'm not sure."

"I see," Adam said. "Perhaps Mr. Wallace's secretary knows. We'd like to speak to her."

Jones maintained his pleasant demeanor. "Certainly. That would be Judith Walker. She's outside Joe's office down the hall. I'll have my girl take you there. Now, is there anything else I can help you with?"

"Actually, there is," Adam said. "We're going to need Mr. Wallace's and Ms. Walker's computers."

"I'm afraid you don't understand, detective, but that won't be possible. Those computers contain sensitive client information. That information is privileged, and—"

"No, Mr. Jones," Adam interrupted. "I don't think *you* understand. This is a murder investigation. You either let us take the computers now, or we just come back with a warrant and a lot of public fuss. Either way, we *will* get access to those computer files."

At $500 an hour, Jones wasn't used to being lectured to. He seemed about to lash out but caught himself. He knew he had little choice but to acquiesce.

"Thank you, sir. Someone from our department will be by in the next hour. And our technicians will know if the computers have been tampered with." Adam and Marcus stood. "Again, we appreciate your help on this. I'm sure we'll need to speak again."

They flipped cards onto Jones' desk and followed Miss Cosmo to Wallace's office.

Wallace's secretary was on the phone but quickly hung up when she saw the detectives. They introduced themselves and jumped into it.

"What can you tell us about Mr. Wallace's frame of mind when he returned from the courtroom Friday afternoon?" Adam asked.

"Well, he was upset. He told me to hold his calls and that he wanted to be left alone."

"That's understandable," Adam said. "That case was a major loss for him and the firm. Did he see anyone before he left the office?"

"Yes. Mr. Jones and Mr. Cole came to his office. They talked for a few minutes, and Mr. Wallace left shortly after that."

"Roughly what time was that?"

"Sometime between 6:00 and 6:30 p.m." She paused and continued, "Probably closer to 6:30 now that I think of it."

"I see. Overall, what kind of boss was he? What was it like working for him?"

The question surprised Judy. "Oh, I don't know. Okay, I guess."

Marcus smiled. "We understand he could be somewhat difficult."

Judy viewed the comment as a welcome opening, one she was more than happy to walk on through. "Yes, he was difficult. He was a good lawyer, but he had his faults."

"Faults?" Marcus pushed. "Faults as in what, Ms. Walker?"

Joe Wallace was dead, and Judy let it all out. "Mr. Wallace was not a nice man. He drank a lot. He wasn't good to his wife. And I know he was in a lot of debt. I got calls every once in a while from people looking to collect money from him."

"Thank you, Ms. Walker," Adam said. "That pretty much confirms what we've heard from others. You said he left Friday afternoon around 6:30. Do you know where he went?"

"Well, I know he had been drinking liquor in his office. When he gets mad and starts drinking like that, he usually goes to a bar named Salty's in North Charleston. I've had to pick him up there a few times when he drank too much and the bartender took his car keys."

Marcus turned to Adam. "I know the place. It's on East Montague."

"Thank you, Ms. Walker," Adam said. "You've been very helpful."

~~~

Twenty-five minutes later, they were at Salty's. It was still morning, and the place was empty—not even a bartender in sight. They bellied up, and Marcus called to the back. "Hello there."

A rough-looking man came lumbering out from a back room and ducked behind the bar. "What can I get you?" They flashed their badges. "Shit, what is it now?"
~~~

"Listen," Adam said, "we're not here to hassle you. I'm Detective Stone, and this is Detective Williams. What's your name?"

"Tony."

"Tony what?" Adam asked.

"White. Tony White."

"All right, Tony White," Adam continued. "I understand Joe Wallace was a regular here. Was he at your bar last Friday night?"

"Why do you wanna know?"

"We're asking the questions," Marcus said. "Now, was Joe Wallace here Friday night?"

"Yeah, he was here."

"Well, seems like he went and got himself murdered after he left."

White looked genuinely shocked. "Jesus Christ. Joe's dead? I didn't know."

"Well, now you do. What time did he get here?"

"I don't remember exactly, but I'd say around 7:00 p.m. or so. Hit the stuff pretty hard that night. As a matter of fact, he got into it with another customer and his girlfriend."

"What, they got into a fight?" Marcus asked.

"Joe was hitting on the girl, and the guy wasn't happy about it. He pushed Joe, and Joe hit him upside his head with a beer bottle. Messed him up."

"Do you happen to know their names?" Marcus asked.

"I don't know the name of the girl, but the guy's name is Bobby McGrath."

"What happened after the fight? Did this McGrath guy consider pressing charges?"

White snickered. "No. He's not the kind of guy to involve the cops in anything. Joe just took off, and as soon as Bobby got it back together, he ran out after him. He never came back, which really pissed me off. First, I let Joe's tab slide just to get him out of here. Then the girl's got no coin to cover the bar tab. Plus, I gave her a twenty for a cab to get her wherever the hell she was going."

"What can you tell us about McGrath?" Adam asked.

"Not a whole lot. He's come in a few times. Never had any trouble with him 'til he got into it with Joe. He works down the road at Cooper Auto Repair. Usually comes on his motorcycle. He rides with the Scorpions."

"We know about the Scorpions," Marcus said. "Did he ride his bike here Friday night?"

White let some time slip by before answering. "No, not that night. I saw him leave in a red Nissan truck. I'm pretty sure it was a Frontier."

"What time did all this go down?"

"Must have been around 9:30 p.m."

"Does the bar have security cameras at the front door?" Adam asked.

"Yeah, front and back doors. There's also one covering the cash register."

"Can you show us the tapes?" Adam asked.

"Sure, but it won't have anything from Friday night. The owner put the system in about twenty years ago, and the tapes record over themselves every forty-eight hours."

"Let's take a look at them anyway," Adam insisted. They did, and White was right—Friday night's video footage was history.

The detectives exchanged a glance. They'd gotten all they could from the bar, at least for now. Marcus tossed a ten-dollar bill and his card on the bar. "That's for the beers we didn't drink. Call me if you think of anything else."

Back in the car, the detectives exchanged another glance. "Well, there's another suspect for us," Adam said. "Mr. Bobby McGrath."

"Yeah, partner, but it'd be nice to start eliminating suspects instead of adding them!"

"That would be nice," Adam agreed. "Let's pay a visit to Mr. McGrath and see what he says about his little encounter with Joe Wallace and his beer bottle."

~~~

Cooper Auto was an older operation on the corner of Rivers and Remount. As they pulled into the parking lot, Marcus noticed a Harley Dyna Super Glide parked around the side. "Looks like he's here."

The shop consisted of a small waiting room and three repair bays. A short bald man in a dark-blue work shirt with "Otto" embroidered on the pocket sat behind the counter eating what
~~~

looked like a mangled meatball sub. He pushed the sandwich aside when Adam and Marcus showed their shields.

"We'd like a few words with Bobby McGrath," Marcus said.

"What's he done now?" the man replied, apparently not at all surprised the police would be there for McGrath.

"Mr. McGrath hasn't done anything wrong, sir. We just have a few questions for him. Shouldn't take long at all."

He pointed to the garage. "He's in the far bay working on the Mazda."

McGrath, covered in grease, some likely from days previous, was underneath a lift working on the Mazda's rear brakes.

"Mr. McGrath, we'd like a few words with you," Marcus said, again showing his detective's shield.

McGrath pulled a dirty rag from his back pocket and wiped his hands. There was a good-sized bandage above his right eye, and the side of his face was discolored from being hit Friday night with the beer bottle.

"I figured you guys would show up." He glanced toward the office window. "I kind of hoped you wouldn't do it here though. It's about that Wallace guy, right?"

"We understand you and Mr. Wallace had a difference of opinion Friday night at Salty's," Marcus said.

"You could say that." He gestured toward his face and bandaged forehead. "The son of a bitch hit me with a beer bottle. Look, I heard Wallace turned up dead. I had nothing to do with that."

"We're not saying you did," Marcus continued. "The bartender said you left right after the altercation and didn't return that night. Where did you go, Mr. McGrath?"

"Listen, I know what this looks like. Sure, I was pissed, but by the time I got outside, the guy was gone."

"You were seen leaving the bar in your truck. Again, where did you go?"

"Sure, I tried to find the asshole. I did take off in my truck, but like I said, he was gone by the time I left the bar."

"If that's the case, why didn't you return to the bar? Your date was there."

McGrath laughed. "My date? No, she's just someone I know. She's a big girl and can take care of herself."

"You never answered my question," Marcus pushed. "Where did you go from there?"

"Back to my place. My head hurt, and I was bleeding."

"Where do you live?"

"Bradley Square Apartments a couple miles down the road on Rivers."

"Did anyone see you after you left the bar and returned to your apartment?"

"No. I took care of my face when I got there. My head hurt like a bitch." He again looked toward the office. "Can I get back to work? I don't want to lose this job."

Marcus gave McGrath one of his cards and said, "All right. We'll be in touch."

~~~
~~~

They were on their way back to Lockwood when Adam asked, "What do you think?"

"He's got a motive and no alibi—not a good combination. The whole thing with him depends on whether or not he got out of Salty's quick enough to actually follow Wallace. If you believe he didn't see Wallace leaving the parking lot, how's he going to find him? He didn't know who he was, where he lived, or where he was going. Plus, we know Wallace was tasered. Would McGrath be carrying a Taser? I doubt it. He could have got ahold of his Scorpion friends, but what good would that do if he didn't know where Wallace was going?"

"You're right," Adam replied. "He's definitely a suspect, but I got the feeling he was telling the truth. We could talk to the Salty's bartender again and nail down how long it was between Wallace leaving and McGrath recovering enough to get outside. But if McGrath's apartment building has security cameras, we can verify whether he actually went back there like he said."

"One way to find out," Marcus said.

They parked in front of the Bradley Square Apartments five minutes later and buzzed the apartment that listed "R. Huang, Superintendent." They buzzed a second time, and the door was opened by an older Asian man.

"Can I help you?"

"Yes, sir," Adam said and showed him his detective shield. "We understand one of your tenants is a man by the name of Robert McGrath."

"Yes, he's in apartment 12."

"Does your building have security cameras?" Adam asked.

"It does. Is Bobby in trouble?" Huang asked.

"No, sir. We were just checking what time he returned to his apartment last Friday night. May we see the tapes?"

"I suppose so. Part of their lease allows management to monitor the building and use the recordings. Come on in."

Adam and Marcus followed Mr. Huang to a computer on a desk in his living room. "Our system is digital. What time do you want to start?"

"I'd say around 9:30 p.m. Friday night would be good," Adam replied.

Huang typed a few numbers into the computer, and four separate screens appeared on the monitor. "The system is motion activated. Just tell me when to stop." He started the recording. The first scene showed a man and a woman parking their car and entering the building at 10:05 p.m. Adam told to Huang to continue. Another man entered the apartment shortly after 10:11 p.m.

A moment later, Marcus pointed and said, "There!" Huang froze the scene showing McGrath exiting a red Nissan truck. "All right, go ahead." He did, and the recording showed McGrath entering the building at 10:20 p.m.

"That's good," Adam said. "Now, please continue the video."

The next scene was a young woman dressed in nurse's scrubs parking her Toyota Corona and entering the building at 11:25 p.m. The tape continued until another woman was seen leaving the building at 6:00 a.m. the next morning. The detectives thanked Mr. Huang and left.

As they turned onto Rivers Road, Marcus said, "Looks like McGrath is off the hook."

"Looks that way," Adam confirmed. "Let's put him on the sidelines until we find something to bring him back into play."

CHAPTER 8

BACK AT LOCKWOOD, Marcus spent some time on the murder book, and Adam updated the timeline on the whiteboard in the conference room. It now read as follows:

Friday: 4:30 p.m.—Guilty verdict Ruiz case
Friday: 5:00 p.m.—Wallace left courthouse
Friday: 6:30 p.m.—Wallace left law office
Friday: 7:00 p.m.—Wallace arrived Salty's bar
Friday: 9:30 p.m.—Wallace left Salty's bar
Friday: 9:30 p.m.—McGrath left Salty's bar
Friday: 10:20 p.m.—McGrath arrives at his apartment
Saturday: 9:00 a.m.—Skulled baggie found Santana's
Saturday: 11:30 a.m.—.38 found Santana's car
Saturday: 12:30 p.m.—Wallace body found at Higgins Pier

They were both at their desks when Merchant called to them from his office. "All right, boys, looks like we caught a break."

They made a beeline to Merchant's office. "I just got off the phone with the manager of the Best Buy on Sam Rittenberg. He reported an abandoned vehicle in his parking lot this morning. Turns out it had been there for a few days … guess whose car it is."

"You got to be kidding!" Adam said. "Wallace's?"

"Yeah, an Audi A-7 registered to Mr. Joseph Wallace. Officers found a cellphone in the car, and our techs had no trouble getting into it. They're still working through its content, but the last call made from the cell was at 9:51 Friday night to a Tanya Scarcella. This Miss Scarcella just happens to live on Dupont Road. And Dupont Road just happens to be located right behind Best Buy. The store's security cameras show a man we assume to be Wallace parking the Audi there at 11:27 Friday night and walking across the lot toward Dupont."

"Looks like we've got a date with Miss Scarcella," Marcus said.

"Hang on," Merchant said. "You need to sit tight for a while. We might not have enough for a warrant to search her house, but it's worth a try. Techs are seeing what they can find on her. Let's wait for that and see what else they get off Wallace's cell. We need to know as much as possible before you interrogate her. I'll let you know when we're ready to move on this. Shouldn't take long."

"All right, Ed," Adam said. "We'll be at our desks. Holler when you get the stuff."

~~~

On the way back to their desks, Adam made a stop in the conference room to update the timeline, and Marcus went to the mailroom to pick up their mail. Adam grabbed a marker and added three additional entries:

Friday: 4:30 p.m.—Guilty verdict Ruiz case
Friday: 5:00 p.m.—Wallace leaves courthouse to office
Friday: 6:30 p.m.—Wallace left law office
Friday: 7:00 p.m.—Wallace arrived Salty's bar
Friday: 9:30 p.m.—Wallace left Salty's bar
Friday: 9:30 p.m.—McGrath left Salty's bar
Friday: 9:51 p.m.—Wallace call to T. Scarcella
Friday: 10:20 p.m.—McGrath arrives at his apartment
Friday: 11:27 p.m.—Audi 7 at Best Buy (Rittenberg)
Friday: 11:27 p.m.—Man (Wallace) leaves car in lot
Saturday: 9:00 a.m.—Skulled baggie found Santana's
Saturday: 11:30 a.m.—.38 found Santana's car
Saturday: 12:30 p.m.—Wallace body found at Higgins Pier

A few minutes later, Marcus tossed some letters on Adam's desk and began going through his own. One envelope caught his eye. It was addressed to the Charleston Police Department with
~~~

"Attention: Detective Williams" in the lower right corner. The letter was handwritten and had no return address. He set the rest of his mail aside and opened the letter.

"Adam, take a look at this." Holding the corner of the letter with two fingers, he held it up so Adam could see. Written in black pen were two words separated by a rough drawing of a knife—*Justicia* and *Venganza*.

"What the hell does that mean?"

"My Spanish isn't that good, but it's good enough. That says *Justice* and *Revenge*."

"Hang on," Adam said. He sifted through his mail and found a letter just like it. He laid it on his desk, careful to touch it as little as possible. "So, what do you think?"

"Miguel Alvarez and the Sinaloa Cartel," Marcus quickly responded. "Listen, don't open that. We need to get these to Merchant."

"Do you think it might have something to do with the Wallace murder?"

"I doubt it. Why in the world would the cartel care about Wallace?"

They slipped the letters into separate evidence bags and took them directly to Merchant. The captain surprised Marcus by coming to a different conclusion. "First of all, I doubt the Sinaloa Cartel had anything to do with this. Granted the loss of their heroin and money hurt, but they'd consider that a cost of doing business. Going after someone in U.S. law enforcement isn't worth the blowback. I doubt we'll find any prints or DNA on those letters, but we'll run them through forensics."

"If it wasn't the cartel then who sent them?" Marcus asked.

"My best guess would be the Posse. Don't forget you guys took out Odell Davis and seriously messed up their distribution network. Plus, Spider Gomez knows you two, and you've been a thorn in the Posse's side for years. Odell Davis was more levelheaded than Spider could ever be. Don't forget in the gang culture violence gets you respect, and the Posse lost a fair amount of it when you busted up their deal with the cartel."

"Whoever sent them might know we're working on the Wallace murder case," Adam offered. "Could it have to do with Wallace and the investigation?"

"I seriously doubt it," Merchant said. "Just because Wallace lost the Ruiz trial doesn't seem like a reason to kill the guy."

"So, where does that leave us?" Marcus said, his frustration obvious.

"I'll have vice put out feelers and see if there's any talk about anyone coming after you two. If there is, we'll know."

"I wish I could say that makes me feel better about the whole thing," Adam said. "Plus, I'm not sure I buy the Posse's role here. They're in the middle of reestablishing themselves in the drug trade. Making a move on anyone on the force wouldn't be worth it."

"Yeah," Marcus agreed. "But who else would have sent us a letter like that?"

"It could have been Alvarez himself," Merchant offered. "These cartel bosses live and die by their reputation, and you guys put a major dent in his."

"What about the Bloods?" Adam asked.

"I doubt they'd have sent their message in Spanish. The Bloods are mostly black dudes. Plus, the more I consider it, the less I think the Bloods are involved in this or Wallace's murder at all. And there's always the chance someone else did this just to mess with you. Don't forget, you two have put a lot of people away. But whoever did it, we need to take it seriously. I'm putting officers on both your houses. And you guys need to take added precautions—for yourselves and your families."

Merchant looked at his watch and continued, "Techs are still working on the phone, and I want to wait on a search warrant for Scarcella's place. I've got someone watching her house. Let's plan on you two seeing the Scarcella woman first thing tomorrow morning."

~~~

It was approaching 10:00 p.m. when Adam told Marcus he was going to make a quick stop at his apartment to check on Tracy and Piper and get something to eat. As he pulled into his apartment complex, he noticed a police cruiser parked across from his unit. He parked his car and started for the cruiser when its driver's side door opened, and an officer got out.

"Detective Stone, I'm Officer Fitzgerald. I have orders to watch your apartment when you're gone."

"Thank you, officer."

"Do you want me to take off, sir?"

"No, I'll only be here for a while and need to get back downtown tonight."
~~~

"Yes, sir. I'll be here until you get back."

"Thanks again, Fitzgerald. Have a good night."

"You do the same, sir."

Adam entered his apartment and found Tracy watching TV in the living room. She seemed surprised to see him.

"How'd it go today?" Adam asked.

"Everything's fine, dear. Are you in for the night?"

"No. I need to get back downtown in an hour or so. Marcus needs a break. Where's Piper?"

"She's in her room."

Adam started toward his daughter's room but stopped when Tracy said, "You missed her teacher conference today."

"Damn it! That was today?"

"It's all right, dear. You were busy. I was there, and the teacher had nothing but good things to say about our girl."

"No, it's not all right. I'll talk to her." He knocked on Piper's bedroom door and then poked his head in.

She was lying on her bed reading her Kindle. "Hi, Dad."

"Hey, sweetheart. I'm really sorry about your conference. I spaced out. How'd it go?"

"Fine. Don't worry. It's no big deal. Granny was there."

"I know, but I should have been there."

"Dad, I know. Don't worry. Really, it's cool. I love you."

"Love you more," Adam said. He quietly shut the door and dropped his head. *Stone, you're an ass.* He returned to the living room and took a seat by the window. He watched light from the streetlamp filter through the trees and throw shadows across the parking lot. He felt a wave of loneliness wash over him.

After a moment, Tracy muted the TV. "Are you all right, dear? What's bothering you?"

A half smile appeared on Adam's face. He had to admit she was as sharp as any cop when it came to reading people. "I'm fine."

Tracy's gaze never left his face. "It's Piper, isn't it? You don't have to talk about it if you don't want to. But if you don't, it'll only get worse."

"I don't know, Tracy. You've been great. It's just that I haven't been much of a dad lately. I'm not talking just about missing her conference. She's thirteen—fourteen in a few months. She's growing up too fast. Before I know it, she'll be off to college. Maybe it's the job. It was okay when Ann was here, but it seems like I'm always gone, and she's growing up without me."

Tracy walked over to Adam, gently lifted his head with her hand, and kissed him on the forehead. "You're a wonderful dad. I know it, and Piper knows it. You're also the best detective I know, so stop worrying about us. Now, I bet you haven't eaten anything, have you? Stay put and I'll make you a sandwich."

"Thanks. Make that to go. I need to get back downtown."

Adam had to smile as he watched Tracy head to the kitchen. *I don't know what I'd do without you.* He knew he should have said it out loud.

CHAPTER 9

ADAM AND MARCUS were in Merchant's office first thing Tuesday morning. Ed had his coat jacket draped over his desk chair and held a steaming cup of coffee in his left hand. A manila folder was open in front of him.

"All right, we got the warrant, and here's what we've have so far on Tanya Scarcella. She's thirty-eight, divorced, works as a waitress at Leonardo's Restaurant."

Adam interrupted, "I know the place. It's on Sam Rittenberg by Ashley Landing. I've never been there though."

"I've eaten there a few times," Merchant offered. "It's a decent place and has good food. It's got a pretty active bar and caters to an older crowd. Anyway, her place on Dupont is a bungalow with a carport. She drives a 2013 Hyundai Accent. We pulled her driver's license." He slid a blown-up copy across his desk.

"She's not bad looking," Marcus remarked.

"I put a patrol car on her place last night. The Hyundai was parked in the carport all night. Being a waitress, she probably works nights and should still be there this morning. We know she's got some sort of connection with Wallace, so go ahead and check her out. Call me with what you get."

They left the station, with Marcus driving an unmarked Impala, and when they rolled up at Scarcella's ten minutes later, the Hyundai was still under the carport. Adam rang the doorbell. No one answered. The drapes were drawn, and it looked dark inside. He knocked several more times without success.

"Let's check the side door," he said. There was another entrance under the carport, and when Adam knocked, they were surprised the door swung partially open.

"Shit," Marcus whispered, "you smell that?" There was no mistaking the rank and pungent odor mixed with a tinge of sickening sweetness. The power of the odor of death was overwhelming. Once experienced, it was a smell no one could ever forget.

Marcus and Adam immediately pulled their Glock 19s, holding them in a two-handed tactical position. Adam eased the door open with his left hand and carefully entered what looked like a mudroom. A washer and dryer were against the right wall, and a few coats hung opposite the machines. A step up led into a small kitchen. Adam, back against the doorjamb, saw two other entrances to the kitchen. One at the far end led to a small dining room, and the other was to his immediate left and opened to the living room. He used hand signals to direct Marcus to the dining room entrance and indicated that he would station himself at the living room opening. Once in position, Adam nodded, and both men moved quickly from the kitchen, firearms extended.

They both froze at the sight of Tanya Scarcella's lifeless body—half seated, half sprawled on a couch. Her nightgown was open, exposing her naked body covered with blood that had congealed to a reddish-brown jelly. Her throat had been sliced open.

Marcus signaled that he'd clear the bedrooms down the hall to his right. A moment later, he called out that the rooms were clear. He reappeared, a hanky covering his nose and mouth. By this time, Adam was kneeling by the body, his jacketed left forearm over his nose.

The body was well into the putrefaction stage. The abdomen, shoulders, and head had turned a greenish color, with the bloating most visible around the face, where the eyes and tongue protruded as the gas inside pushed out. The legs showed a bluish-purple lividity discoloration with the settling and pooling of blood.

Adam started to gag. "Let's get out of here!" They rushed out through the carport and Adam said, "I'll call 911."

"Wait," Marcus said. "I think we should call Merchant first."

Adam nodded his agreement and made the call. Merchant's secretary, Gail, answered.

"Gail, it's Adam Stone. I need to talk to Ed."

"He's in a meeting, detective. Can I take a message?"

"I need to talk to him now. Just tell him I'm on the line. He'll take it."

Gail patched him through, and Merchant answered.

"Ed, we're at Scarcella's house. She's dead. Throat cut."

"Hang on." Adam could hear Merchant's muffled voice telling whoever was in his office to leave and shut the door. "All right, tell me what you've got."

He quickly reported how they'd found Scarcella and the condition of the body. "Ed, she's been dead for days."

"All right. You two stay put. I'll send units and EMS out there and advise forensics and the coroner. Keep the area clear until they get there. I'm coming too."

Adam relayed Merchant's instructions to his partner. Still breathing heavily, Marcus said, "Jesus Christ, I just bought this suit!" After twenty years on the force, both had been to countless scenes like they'd just witnessed. They also knew that it was virtually impossible to get the repugnant smell of death from their clothes.

While waiting for a cruiser to arrive, Marcus inspected the outside of the house for possible points of entry. Nothing seemed amiss. Adam retrieved a small box from the Impala with crimes scene gloves and plastic shoe covers. The first cruiser pulled up a few minutes later, and Marcus directed it to park in the street. Adam recognized the two officers exiting the patrol car but couldn't recall their names. The older of the two— obviously the lead—introduced himself as Officer Clark and his partner, Officer Hunter.

"We got a report of a 10-67," Clark said. "Where's the body, sir?"

Marcus paid no attention to Clark's question and directed him to secure tape across the front door and around the carport. "And when you're finished, keep civilians away from the house."

A few minutes later, the bright-yellow tape was in place, and a few neighbors had gathered on the sidewalk. Clark was in the process of dispersing them. Marcus had his flashlight out and was inspecting the interior of the Hyundai when Hunter approached.

"Sir, I've only been on the force for six months. I've never been to a homicide. Would it be possible to get inside?"

Hunter was about 5' 7" and not much more than 160. Marcus looked down at him. "So, you want to see the dead body? I take it you've never seen one."

"No, sir, not like this. This is my first murder."

Marcus was about to say something when forensics pulled up across the street followed by a blue-and-yellow EMS van. Marcus gave Hunter a pair of crime scene gloves and booties. "Put these on when I tell you to." He pointed to the carport entrance. "Once forensic assesses the scene, you can take a look, but for God's sake, don't touch anything."

"Yes, sir. I mean no, sir. I won't."

Marcus remembered his first murder scene. It was during his initial year as a patrol officer when he and his partner responded to a domestic dispute. They arrived at the apartment and found that the woman had been sprayed with bullets; the man had taken his own life by swallowing one. The nightmares lasted for weeks. Since then, he'd lost track of the dead bodies he'd seen over the last twenty years, but he never forgot the faces.

Two paramedics approached Marcus. He told them the body was long dead but to sit tight—the coroner might need help moving it.

Adam was off the phone and updating CSI on the situation inside. There were three techs—two with large metal cases and one with a backpack and camera. All of them were draped in the required amount of plastic as they followed Adam into the house.

Adam reappeared about five minutes later, a grim look on his face. Marcus nodded at the rookie and pointed to the carport entrance. "Your turn, Hunter."

Adam waved the young officer over and gave Marcus a sardonic smile. "His first time?" Adam asked. Marcus nodded. "All right. We're going in."

Adam reentered the house followed by the rookie. A few minutes later, Hunter appeared, gloved hands covering his mouth. Marcus pointed to the backyard beyond the yellow tape. "Not here, son!" Hunter ran under the tape and vomited.

About thirty minutes later, Merchant and O'Sullivan arrived and were being appraised of the situation. "Well, Detective Williams," O'Sullivan said, "looks like you brought me another customer. When can I meet him?"

"The techs should be about finished, and him is a her, by the way. Come on, I'll introduce you to the late Ms. Tanya Scarcella."

It took O'Sullivan only ten minutes to inspect the body, assess the surroundings, and formally certify Scarcella's death. She had the EMS techs bag the body and deposit it in the coroner's van.

"Okay, fellas. I'll wait for the autopsy, but I think there's a good chance you've got two homicides and one killer. This throat was also cut with a serrated blade, and the pattern of the incision matches Wallace's. Based on the condition of the body, it looks like she and Wallace were killed within the same general time period. Two for the price of one."

It was now midmorning, and the forensic techs were completing their investigation. Workers from BIO-ONE, a company specializing in homicide and other extreme cleanups, had arrived and were waiting for the techs to finish so they could fumigate and sanitize the inside of Scarcella's house.

"All right, detectives," Merchant said, "I need to get back. I want you two at Leonardo's. Find out what you can. Did Scarcella work Friday night? Did Wallace frequent the restaurant? What kind of relationship did they have?" Merchant was getting into his car but stopped and turned back with a smile. "Oh, and also see if the guys from BIO-ONE can do anything about your clothes. You two smell like shit."

~~~

There were only a few cars parked at Leonardo's when Adam and Marcus arrived. The front door was locked. Marcus knocked, and a moment later, a middle-aged woman appeared—
~~~

the smell of old grease wafting out with her—and said they weren't open yet.

Marcus flipped open his detective shield. "We need to speak with the manager."

"Yes, sir. He's in the back. Come on in, and I'll get him."

The restaurant was surprisingly spacious and well appointed. About fourteen or fifteen tables were arranged in the dining area to the right of the maître d' station. A long mahogany bar ran along the far-right wall. The place had an Italian feel— red-checkered tablecloths and lots of leather. The dark paneled walls were adorned with photos of the Tuscany landscape.

A minute or two later, a silver-haired man with a noticeable paunch made his way over from the bar area. "Gentlemen, I'm Frank Roggiero. What can I do for you?"

"We just have a few questions about one of your waitresses, Ms. Tanya Scarcella," Adam said.

"Tanya? Is she okay? I've been trying to get ahold of her. She missed her last two shifts, Saturday and last night. That's not like her. Has something happened?"

Marcus looked at Adam and nodded. "I'm sorry, Mr. Roggiero," Adam continued, "but we found her body this morning. I'm afraid she's dead."

Roggiero's eyes widened—the look of someone truly affected by death. "Oh God! Dead? What happened?"

"Like I said, we discovered her body this morning at her house. When was the last time you saw her?"

Roggiero was deeply shaken. "What? Oh yeah. Friday night. She worked her section until around 11:00 p.m. Busy night."

"So, would it be safe to say she left the restaurant a little after that?"

"Yeah, we stop taking dinner orders around 10:00 p.m. Our table waitresses are usually out of here between 10:30 and 11:00, depending on the crowd."

Adam nodded. "We also learned that a Mr. Joseph Wallace sometimes eats here. Was he here Friday night?"

Roggiero paused, now looking somewhat defensive. "You mean the lawyer? What's he got to do with this?"

Adam dug in. "Friday night, Mr. Roggiero. Was Mr. Wallace here at your restaurant this past Friday night?"

"Yeah. Joe stopped in Friday. I remember because he seemed upset and was a bit unsteady."

"What time would you say he arrived that night, sir?"

Roggiero thought for a moment. "It was later. The dinner crowd was thinning, and it was too late to order food. He just had a drink at the bar. I'd say he got here around 10:30 or so? Is Joe all right?"

"No, Mr. Roggiero, Mr. Wallace is not all right. He was found dead several days ago. We're treating both his and Ms. Scarcella's deaths as homicides."

"Jesus, they were murdered! You think the same person killed both of them?"

"We don't know," Adam said. "At least, not as of yet. Now, I'm assuming Ms. Scarcella knew Mr. Wallace. Is that correct?"

Roggiero looked like he was about to tip over and ball himself up in the booth. "Yes, Joe knew Tanya. He always sat in her section."

"Did Mr. Wallace and Ms. Scarcella have a relationship outside the restaurant? Were they seeing each other?"

Roggiero stiffened. "We discourage our employees from seeing customers outside of the restaurant. It's bad for business. Listen, what's going on here?" He paused and took a deep breath. "Sorry, I guess I'm still processing the news. It's just she was one of my best waitresses, and people are always making awful assumptions about a restaurant's staff. They do their job and refill a customer's water glass, and all of a sudden they're having an affair."

"I really am sorry for your loss, but there are some details from the case that lead us to suspect they might have been involved. So, I'll ask again—any chance their relationship was less, uh, professional outside the restaurant?"

Roggiero sighed. "Yeah, all right. They were seeing each other, but they were good at keeping everything on the up and up inside my place. They always acted like, you know, just like a waitress and a customer."

"How did you know they were seeing each other?" Adam asked.

"I'm the manager. I know everything that goes on around here. I've seen Tanya get into Joe's car plenty of times after work. Joe usually comes in around 9:30 or 10:00 and leaves about the time Tanya finishes up."

"All right, Mr. Roggiero," Adam continued, "you've been helpful, and we appreciate that. Now what time did Wallace leave here Friday?"

"I remember I said good night to him a little after 11:00."

"Who was bartending that night?"

"That would be Jimmy Esposito. He gets in at 4:00 p.m. and works the dinner and late-night crowd."

"I see. We'll be back to speak with Mr. Esposito."

~~~

Back in the bullpen, Adam updated the timeline of Wallace's murder by adding:

Friday: 4:30 p.m.—Guilty verdict Ruiz case

Friday: 5:00 p.m.—Wallace leaves courthouse to office

Friday: 6:30 p.m.—Wallace left law office

Friday: 7:00 p.m.—Wallace arrived Salty's bar

Friday: 9:30 p.m.—Wallace left Salty's bar

Friday: 9:30 p.m.—McGrath left Salty's bar

Friday: 9:51 p.m.—Wallace call to Tanya Scarcella

Friday: 10:20 p.m.—McGrath arrives at his apartment

Friday: 10:30 p.m.—Wallace arrive Leonardo's Restaurant

Friday: 11:27 p.m.—Audi 7 parked at Best Buy (Rittenberg)

Friday: 11:27 p.m.—Man (assume Wallace) leaves car—walks toward Dupont Road

Saturday: 9:00 a.m.—Skulled baggie found Santana's

Saturday: 11:30 a.m.—.38 found Santana's car

Saturday: 12:30 p.m.—Wallace body found at Higgins Pier

Tuesday: 9:00 a.m.—Scarcella's body found at her home
~~~

Marcus joined him in the conference room. Adam removed the spiral notebook he used for field notes and checked his watch. "All right, partner, let's organize what we've got so far and then give Merchant an update."

Marcus pulled out his own notebook. "Let's start with last Friday afternoon. We know Wallace returned to his office after the Ruiz verdict between 5:00 and 5:30. His secretary said he met with two partners and left the office around 6:30. Then he drove his Audi to Salty's and spent a few hours drinking before getting into it with Bobby McGrath. The bartender said he left the bar about 9:30 and so did McGrath. We don't know if McGrath followed him.

"We do know Wallace called the waitress at 9:51 that night, and Roggiero said he got to Leonardo's close to 10:30. Roggiero also said Wallace left the restaurant shortly after 11:00, about the same time the waitress did. You got to figure he followed Scarcella, for some reason parked his Audi in the Best Buy lot and walked to her house on Dupont."

"Why would he park his car at Best Buy?" Adam asked. "He didn't care much whether or not Elizabeth or the Buckleys knew he was messing around on the side."

"Who knows?" Marcus answered. "We know he was drunk. Plus, he left his cellphone in the car." Marcus paused, allowing Adam to update all the timeline notes before he continued. "We didn't discover Scarcella's body until this morning. That's almost four days or so after she was murdered, which O'Sullivan said was roughly the same time Wallace was killed. Both their throats were cut with a serrated blade. Considering the similarities and their involvement with each other, it's safe to assume we're looking at the same killer."

"Got it," Adam said.

When they arrived at Merchant's office, they shared the timeline and then took a deep dive into the suspect list. The prime suspects were Nick Santoro and the Chicago mob and Noah Buckley. It was decided that Bobby McGrath could be eliminated from consideration because Wallace was gone from the bar well before McGrath had a chance to follow him, and security cameras recorded him returning to his apartment at 10:20 Friday night. They discussed the Bloods and the Posse—concluding that the Bloods were most likely no longer in the picture, and the Posse was becoming less of a suspect than previously thought. They also discussed the $100 bill in Wallace's throat and the possibility that someone may have put a professional contract out on him.

"Okay," Merchant said. "There's no evidence that the Scarcella woman was being targeted by anyone. I doubt any of the suspects even knew who she was. She was probably collateral damage—wrong place, wrong time—so you need to focus on Wallace. None of his blood was found in her house, and there is evidence he was tasered, killed somewhere else, and dumped in the river. Hell, maybe Wallace killed her himself. There's still a lot of maybes. Recheck alibis and revisit everyone you've already interviewed—look for inconsistencies and press them. Does O'Sullivan have anything else from the lab or forensics?"

"Yeah, for Wallace but nothing yet for Scarcella," Marcus replied. "Wallace had alcohol and cocaine in his system. No luck lifting prints, though, and O'Sullivan doubts they'd recover any DNA. We should get the lab results on Scarcella any time now."

"Go ahead and cycle back through Noah Buckley, but be careful," Merchant warned. "He's connected at the hip with our mayor and a lot of city and state politicians. And I asked you before, but why haven't you interviewed the wife, Elizabeth Wallace? The clock is running."

"We told you she's been out of the country and hasn't answered our calls," Adam explained. "She's flying back to Charleston late tonight or early tomorrow morning."

"I can see where she might be another piece of the puzzle," Merchant said. "Just make sure you interview her as soon as she's back in town."

It had been a long day, and you could hear the vexation in Adam's voice. "We're on it, Ed—first thing tomorrow morning."

CHAPTER 10

ADAM WAS BACK in the bullpen before 7:00 a.m. Wednesday morning and wasn't surprised to find Marcus already working—papers covering his desk and the murder book open in front of him.

Adam gave him one of the lattes and a blueberry scone he'd picked up at the Coffee Cup on his way downtown.

"Thanks. I could use some caffeine. It feels like I just left this place."

"You got that right."

Adam was taking the top off his latte when Captain Merchant appeared. "I just got off the phone with the DA. She found out that Wallace will be cremated, and his remains are to be buried in a plot at Holy Cross Cemetery on James Island." Merchant smiled and continued, "Now, that wouldn't be at all interesting except for the fact that the Buckleys have a family plot at Magnolia Cemetery on the Peninsula."

Adam returned the smile. "I guess that's not too surprising. They didn't like Wallace when he was alive, and they haven't changed their minds now that he's dead. When's the funeral?"

"Tomorrow morning at 10:00," Merchant replied. "And I want you two there. Get the license plate numbers and make a note of everyone who attends."

"Got it," Marcus said. After the captain left, he told Adam he'd received a message from Judge Roberts' clerk saying the warrants for the phone and bank records were ready. "I also got one from O'Sullivan. Wallace's autopsy results are ready to be picked up. I'll catch up with things around here and pick up the warrants later this morning. Why don't you go ahead and get the autopsy report and interview Elizabeth Wallace? We can meet back here when you're finished with Wallace."

~~~

Adam retrieved Elizabeth Wallace's cell number he'd gotten from her maid and made the call. It rang several times before a sleepy voice answered, "Who is this?"

"Hello, Mrs. Wallace. This is Detective Stone of the Charleston Police Department. I'm calling to arrange ..."

"For heaven's sake! Do you know what time it is?"

"Yes, ma'am. I apologize for calling this early, but it's important that I meet with you as soon as possible. It's concerning your husband's death. My partner and I are investigating ..."
~~~

Adam was interrupted again. "Can't this wait?"

"No, ma'am, it can't!" Adam answered, his voice more emphatic. "Your husband was murdered. This is a homicide investigation."

"Hold on a second," she said. Adam heard rustling in the background before she was back on the line, her tone softened. "I'm sorry I snapped at you. It's just that I flew in late last night, and I've hardly slept."

"I understand, Mrs. Wallace. I appreciate this is a very difficult and emotional time. But we do need your help—it's critical. I won't need much of your time. When are you available today?"

"I have a luncheon at noon, and my father wants me to meet his lawyers this afternoon to sign some papers. I'll be having dinner at my parents' house tonight. Can you stop by there this evening?"

"I'm afraid not, Mrs. Wallace. I need to speak to you without your mother and father present. I could stop by your house this morning. Again, this won't take long at all."

There was a pause of several seconds. Adam thought he heard voices in the background. Finally, Elizabeth responded, "I suppose, but I need to leave no later than 11:30. Can you stop by at 9:30?"

"Yes, that will work, and thank you for your patience. We'll do everything possible to find out what happened to your husband. I'll be by to see you at 9:30."

Adam hung up and groaned. "These people don't even pretend to care that Joe Wallace had his throat slit."

"Yeah," Marcus said. "Sounded like you had to work to get that one done."

"I'm pretty sure I woke her up. I thought I heard voices in the background. She might have been talking to someone. She wasn't happy about meeting, but she agreed just as long as it didn't interrupt her luncheon."

"It sounds like she might not be all that helpful," Marcus observed.

~~~

Adam took an unmarked Crown Vic from the carpool and made the ten-mile drive to the Charleston County morgue. With the exception of the DNA analysis, the Scarcella autopsy report was ready to pick up.

Alice O'Sullivan met Adam at the front door and was walking him back to her office when he asked, "How's business, Alice?"

"Excellent! The fine people of Charleston continue to be steady customers of mine. How's the Wallace case going?"

"Nothing too solid yet. We're hoping Scarcella's autopsy might give us something to work with."

"I don't want to burst your bubble, detective, but I don't think I found a whole lot that'll help."

They settled into her office, and she slid the report across her spotless desk—everything in there always seemed like it had just been sprayed down with Lysol.

"Thanks, Alice. Give me the highlights."
~~~

"First off, I'd say the killer was most likely wearing gloves. As you'd expect, most of the prints forensics found in the house were Scarcella's. They did find several of Wallace's prints, but there's no way of knowing if they were left that night. Forensics only found her prints on her clothes. Lifting prints off human skin is extremely difficult. They tried but had no luck. The only blood found was hers, so whoever killed Wallace didn't do it there. Remember the surface skin was burned around the two puncture marks on Wallace's chest. So, if he was at Scarcella's that night, he was likely tasered and given some form of chemical compound to render him unconscious. There were no traces of anesthetic drugs in either of their bodies, but that's not surprising. It's difficult to find residue from these compounds after twenty-four to forty-eight hours."

"Were you able to determine whether she had intercourse that night?"

"No. I found no semen. No other indications. Anyway, it's tough to tell forty-eight hours after death."

"Drugs or alcohol?"

"Alcohol, yes, but that doesn't tell us much. It's hard to estimate pre-death alcohol levels. Our bodies process alcohol and break it down into harmless substances over time. But corpses sometimes contain self-generated alcohol created by bacteria, and the alcohol level can rise as the body decays. Don't forget Ms. Scarcella had been dead for almost four days before you found her."

Adam wasn't really expecting all that much, but he was still disappointed. He picked up the folder and thanked Alice.

"Sorry I couldn't help you out on this one, Adam."

It was approaching 9:00 a.m. by the time Adam made it to Daniel Island. He had another half hour to kill before seeing Elizabeth Wallace and decided to stop in one of the Starbucks on the island. He ordered a plain black coffee and found a seat by the front window. He glanced out the window just in time to see a car swerve—barely missing a woman jogging across the street. He wondered if the woman ever thought about being in the wrong place at the wrong time. He closed his eyes and tried to visualize the scene that played out in Scarcella's house that night.

Wallace follows Scarcella out of Leonardo's around 11:00 p.m. She knows him well enough to see that something's wrong—he's unsteady, and his clothes are disheveled. Maybe he's not the only man she entertains. Is Wallace paying her? She's a waitress—she could use the money. She tells Joe to follow her home. What she doesn't know is that someone else is following Joe. She's waiting for him at the door. "Come on in, baby. Get yourself a drink while I freshen up." She puts on a see-through negligee and robe. But when she comes out of the bedroom, Joe's unconscious on the floor. She doesn't even see who clubs her in the back of her head. She's carried to the couch, and that's where she takes her last breath. Wrong place, wrong time.

~~~

Adam left Starbucks and arrived at the Wallace residence at 9:30 a.m.
~~~

"Good morning, sir. Come in. Mrs. Wallace is expecting you." The same maid he'd met during his first visit asked Adam to have a seat in the living room. "I'll let Mrs. Wallace know you are here."

The house wasn't as large or as opulent as the Buckleys', but it was still impressive. It backed up to the Wando River and had a dock where a good-sized powerboat rested on a lift. Adam wondered what would happen to the boat—it had to be Joe's, and he wasn't coming back to kick up waves up and down the river. He doubted Elizabeth Wallace would have much use for it. He waited about five minutes before the maid retrieved him. "Mrs. Wallace will see you now. If you will come with me, please?"

Adam followed her down a long hallway to the library, where bookcases lined the mahogany-paneled walls; an ornate ebony desk served as the room's focal point. Elizabeth was seated behind the desk and stood when Adam entered.

"Hello, Detective Stone." Before Adam could respond, she turned toward a short man in a dark suit standing next to one of the bookcases—Adam had totally missed him. "This is Mr. Turner."

"Good morning, sir," the man said. "I'm Thomas Turner, a friend of the family. I'll be sitting in on your interview."

Adam was not expecting this and paused for a moment. "Are you saying you're Mrs. Wallace's attorney?"

"I've done some legal work for Elizabeth in the past. I'm just here to monitor the meeting."

"Tom thought it would be a good idea when I told him you were coming over," Elizabeth offered.

Adam wasn't pleased but couldn't do much about it. "All right then. Mrs. Wallace, let's start with your trip. I understand you were gone for the past week or so. Where did you go, and when were you scheduled to return?"

"Let me see. I was on a cruise to Nassau with some friends. We left almost two weeks ago and had planned on returning tomorrow."

"I see. Do you often vacation without your husband?"

"Excuse me, detective," Turner interrupted. "I don't see how that has anything to do with your investigation."

Adam fixed his gaze on Turner for a few seconds before speaking. "You can be part of this interview if Mrs. Wallace wishes you to. This is a homicide investigation, and there are certain questions that need to be answered. I realize you may have represented Mrs. Wallace, but you're going to have to allow me to conduct the interview. Is that clear?"

Turner's expression didn't shift, but his face reddened. He looked to be on the verge of objecting but bit his tongue.

Adam returned his attention to Elizabeth. "As I was saying, Mrs. Wallace, did you often travel without your husband?"

"Well, let me just say that Joseph and I grew to have different interests. I didn't especially enjoy the activities he chose to pursue, and I doubt he enjoyed mine."

"I understand," Adam said. "Did you happen to speak with your husband while you were gone?"

"No."

"Had your husband seemed overly worried or nervous about anything recently? Did he tell you about any problems at work or in his personal relationships?"

Elizabeth smiled. "We rarely discussed his work, and I chose not to involve myself in what you call his 'personal relationships.'"

"How about his financial situation? Did he talk about any money problems?"

"No," she answered. "I mean, no more than usual. Joseph was never very good with money, and it's no secret that he tended to gamble quite a lot. He'd sometimes get in over his head, and Daddy and I would have to help him out."

"I see. Did he have enemies? Anyone who may have wanted to do him harm?"

Elizabeth gave a sarcastic laugh. "My husband had a superiority complex, detective. He wasn't very nice to people, and I'm sure he had his share of adversaries. Plus, he was a defense attorney and often represented people who did bad things—that's a good way to make enemies."

"I see. But can you think of specific people who would have wanted to hurt him?"

"No. Nobody specific."

Adam spent the next twenty-five minutes questioning her about Joe's work at the firm, the extent of his gambling, and whether he exhibited problems with alcohol or drugs. She answered all the questions with complete passivity. At best, she seemed indifferent about her husband's death.

Mr. Turner was quiet throughout the balance of questioning, but he'd clearly remained livid and seemed upset when the interview ended without getting to return the favor with a silver-tongued joust.

Elizabeth checked her watch and stood. "I'm afraid that's all the time I have for you, detective. Come, I'll walk you to the door."

Elizabeth was watching Adam get into his car when Turner joined her. Her eyes were still focused on the detective when she smiled and said, "Well, Tom, how'd I do?"

"You did well, dear. But I was a bit concerned about the way you described your relationship with Joe. It came off fairly harsh."

"Oh, you do, do you? It's no secret what kind of man Joe was. What do you think the detective would have thought if I played the confused and distraught wife who just lost the love of her life?"

"You're right. I just think you should be careful around Stone. He seemed pretty sharp." Turner slid his arm around her waist.

"I'm always careful," she responded. "You of all people should know that."

He pulled her close, and they watched Adam Stone back the Crown Vic out of her driveway and disappear down Ocean Point Drive.

~~~
~~~

Marcus had picked up the warrants and met up with Adam back at the station. Armed with bank warrants, they drove to the Wells Fargo office in Mount Pleasant to serve the warrants on the Buckleys' banking records. They did the same for the Wallaces' at the Daniel Island branch of South State Bank. The balance of most of the afternoon was spent serving the phone warrants to various locations to collect the records, which would be ready as early as the following day.

They returned to Lockwood in time to update Chief Taylor on the progress—or lack thereof—on both murder cases. The fact that it had been five days since the Wallace murder was not lost on Chief Taylor. In medicine, they call it "the Critical Hour." In criminal investigations, they call it "the First 48." Ask any detective, and they will tell you that if they haven't made an arrest within the first forty-eight hours after a murder, their chances of solving the case are cut in half. And it's also true that if the case is not cracked in the first two weeks, it will probably never be solved.

When they finished the update, the chief's voice grew somber. "Adam, Covell and Simmons were trailing Santana this morning when he drove over the Johns Island Connector and pulled into your apartment complex. Now, we know it's not unusual for these gangs to keep track of the detectives investigating them, but the Posse is reestablishing ties with the Sinaloa Cartel, and it's safe to say that neither of those groups have a soft spot for you guys. I'm going to order backups for Officers Fitzgerald and Rodriguez. I want someone watching your homes 24/7."

The meeting broke up, and Adam and Marcus were back in the bullpen discussing the Santana drive-by of Adam's apartment and their frustration with the lack of progress Merchant had made. They didn't think they could afford to continue waiting on Merchant's people and decided to make a move themselves.

"I'll tell you what," Adam said. "Why don't you get ahold of Mikey—see if he's heard anything about the Wallace murder."

Like any good cop, Marcus had assembled his own set of snitches over the years within the criminal community. As long as the crime committed wasn't murder or terrorism, cops would sometimes let it slide. Then they'd generate quid pro quos, a common deal between criminals and police officers—dangling potential charges in exchange for information. And these snitches were often founts of intel. Cops relied on them and did their best to preserve the flow. It was understood that the informants would pay dearly if it was discovered they were working with law enforcement.

One of these snitches was a member of the Posse by the name of Mikey Brown. Last year, Marcus had used Brown to uncover information on Miguel Alvarez and the Sinaloa Cartel's work smuggling heroin into Charleston.

"Yeah, I can do that," Marcus agreed. "I can also see if he's heard any plans about us—somebody sent us those letters." Marcus picked up his desk phone and dialed. He waited a moment and then said, "Gee, sorry. I must have punched in the wrong number." He hung up.

A moment later, his cell rang, and Marcus answered. "Yeah. Can you talk?" He told Mikey what he needed to know about

Wallace and then waited for a moment. "I also need to know if you've heard talk about a hit put out on Adam Stone and me." Another pause. "Yeah, well, I could care less about that. Do what I told you to do, and I'll meet you at our regular place tomorrow morning at 8:00."

Marcus hung up and Adam asked, "What did Mikey say?"

"He doesn't know much, but he said he'll find out."

"Can you trust him? Remember I got shot by one of my snitches last year."

"I hear you," Marcus said. "I couldn't forget that. But Mikey's always been pretty straight with me, and he knows I'll take him down if he isn't."

"Listen, that gives me an idea," Adam said. "I haven't seen Chester in a while. Maybe he's got information too."

One of Adam's informants was a computer hacker named Chester Wood. Wood lived in the dark side of the web, generally under the employ of various organized crime elements in Charleston. A few years ago, he was hired by some underworld types to plant child pornography in the work computer of a local politician. But when Chester went to plant the porn, he found plenty of incriminating evidence already there. So, he just tipped off the cops and one more political career came to an embarrassing end. Adam made sure that Chester never really had to explain what he was doing inside that computer in the first place and, by doing so, added a world-class hacker to his stable of snitches.

Chester lived with his squirrely little girlfriend, Nora, near the abandoned Navy Shipyards in an old bodega that had been converted into a one-bedroom apartment. Adam never bothered to check to see if Chester was at his place. The only time he ever left was to pick up fast food or buy some sophisticated piece of computer hardware.

The apartment windows were blackened and barred, the formerly white walls of the building now a dingy gray. Adam knocked on the metal door and waited. Finally, he heard a series of locks clicking. Then the door opened slightly, still held by a security chain.

"Who's there?"

"Nora. It's Adam."

He could hear a high-pitched giggle. "What's the secret password?"

"Quit messing around, Nora, and open the damn door."

The security chain was released, and the door swung open. As soon as Adam was inside, Nora relocked the door. "I'd be careful if I were you. Chester's in one of his moods."

The room was dim, and it took a moment for his eyes to adjust. A red beanbag chair slumped against the far wall, the rest of the living room filled with various gadgetry—all of it connected by a myriad of switches and cables crisscrossing the floor. There was little room to walk, much less sit. Behind one of three monitors, lit by its glow, sat Chester Wood. He fit the image of a prototypical hacker—dark eyes inset in a thin face, long black hair under a hooded gray sweatshirt, a liter of Pepsi sitting on the table next to his main keyboard. He continued to peck away, giving no notice to Adam.

"Chester," Adam said, "stop doing whatever it is you're doing." He continued to type, seemingly oblivious to Adam's presence. Adam navigated his way through the maze of cables to an electrical outlet. He bent down and grabbed the large cable plugged into the outlet. "Gee, I wonder what would happen if I pulled this plug?"

Chester immediately stopped typing. "All right, all right! What do you need now, Stone?"

"You can start by dropping the attitude."

Chester finally looked at Adam. "Sorry, Stone, but I'm really backed up here."

"You're about to get even more backed up." Adam told him about the Ruiz verdict and how the defense attorney came floating down the river a short time later.

Chester already knew this. Adam wasn't surprised. Chester had worked for most of the criminal organizations in Charleston and was wired in with his own sources. Few people knew the players or the playing field better than Chester Wood.

"You heard anything about who might have taken out Wallace?" Adam asked.

"Nothing concrete. Only that he owed a lot of money to Nick Santoro and his friends in Chicago. That's not a very healthy situation to be in."

"How about my partner and me? Anyone planning on coming after us?"

"Nothing lately. But it wouldn't surprise me."

"That's comforting," Adam mumbled.

"Anything else, Stone?" Chester pointed at his monitor. "I got deadlines you know."

"Yeah, one more thing. I need you to check out a lawyer in Charleston by the name of Tom Turner."

There was a muffled laugh and Chester said, "The Dishonorable Thomas J. Turner, Esquire? Everybody knows him."

"What do you mean?"

"Turner's got a shady rep," Chester answered. "He does mostly personal injury cases, and the word on the street is that he's connected."

"Connected as in what?" Adam questioned.

"As in Nick Santoro, detective. I hope you aren't thinking of hiring Turner."

"No, Chester, I'm not. I just ran into him the other day."

"Are you telling me he's involved in the Wallace thing?"

"I'm not telling you anything. I just want your take on the guy."

"Well, my take is that if you've met him, I suggest you wash your hands. Seriously, I'd be careful around him. That's all."

"Yeah, I sort of got the same feeling," Adam said. "Have you heard anything about Miguel Alvarez being in Charleston lately?"

"Nope. But if he is, I figure something big is goin' down."

~~~
~~~

After Adam left for Chester's place, Marcus decided to contact an old friend who worked on the FBI's UCR database. The Uniform Crime Reporting program is a nationwide system used by federal, state, and local law enforcement agencies to report specific information describing crimes committed in their jurisdiction. The data is compiled to compare to specific characteristics of a crime that took place in one jurisdiction with those that occurred in other parts of the country.

Marcus described certain characteristics present in Joe Wallace's murder, including the use of a Taser, the serrated knife blade, the manner in which the throat was cut, the dumping of the victim in a body of water, and the discovery of the $100 bill, among other things. Few crimes committed are exact matches; however, the system will generate historical crimes meeting a reasonable number of similar characteristics as the crime being investigated.

It took a little over thirty minutes for Marcus to answer the questions required by the CRU program and allow the FBI agent to enter the data into the computer. The results were interesting, to say the least. There were eight murders in the historical database that matched the required number of similar murder characteristics to those present in Wallace's murder. Two on the West Coast; one in the Kansas City area; two in Chicago; one in Columbia, South Carolina; and two in New York City. Only two of the eight were ever solved—one in New York City and one in Chicago. The interesting part was that a member of the South Side Outfit—another name for the Chicago's mafia—was tried and convicted in the murder of a local city politician who headed an investigation into a labor union controlled by the Outfit. The politician's body was found in Lake Michigan, his neck cut with a serrated blade, and a $100 bill was lodged in his throat.

Marcus was in the conference room when Adam returned from seeing Chester. Marcus had to control his excitement listening to Adam describe what he'd learned in his meeting. Finally, he was able to tell Adam of his call to the UCR and what he'd learned—the connection between the killing of the politician in Chicago and Joe Wallace's murder was clear. Charleston's Nick Santoro is the nephew of Chicago's Eddie Santoro, a lieutenant in the South Side Outfit. "Jesus, Marcus, I need a minute to get my head around this. So, you're saying that the Chicago mafia might be involved in the murder of Joe Wallace? Damn, brother, that's some awesome detective work!"

"I'm not saying it, Adam. The UCR data tells the story. It sure looks like someone in the Santoro family might be behind it."

Adam thought a moment. "All right, this is hard evidence for us, but only circumstantial, at best, for DA Stewart. We need a hell of a lot more than just this connection—as good as it is."

"You're right," Marcus said, a bit of the air leaking out of his balloon. "We've got those phone records. I say we get started on them. Who knows, maybe there's a connection to the murderer somewhere in there."

Phone records for both the Wallaces and the Buckleys documented the calls made to and from their individual cellphones as well as their landlines. The records had been downloaded onto flash drives, which allowed for a variety of filters to be applied when analyzing the data.

Adam worked on Joe and Elizabeth Wallace's calls, and Marcus began scrutinizing the ones for Noah and Shelly Buckley. It was decided they would begin by creating a simple list of all phone numbers appearing in the files regardless of the number of times the number appeared. As long as a landline was still active, there would be no problem immediately accessing the name of the owner and location of the phone. And if the sim card were still in a cellphone and the phone itself had not been destroyed, the cell carrier could identify all incoming and outgoing telephone numbers and the date, time, and duration of the conversation. And because calls were sent through a network of cell towers, the general location of the calls could be identified even if a burner phone was used.

It was a time-consuming task to identify and remove those calls made or received in what could be considered the normal course of everyday conversations. For example, calls made to beauty salons, country clubs, close friends, and neighbors, as well as other "everyday" phone numbers, were set aside.

As the hours passed, Adam found it more difficult to concentrate on the task at hand. His mind continued to slide back to thoughts of Piper and Tracy. Was Santana watching his apartment? Were they safe? What were they thinking when they looked out of the window and saw Officer Fitzgerald and his patrol car parked outside their apartment? Tracy had lost her daughter and Piper her mom when Ann was murdered two years ago. He felt the weight of responsibility dragging him down

Before he knew it, it was after midnight, and they were still not even halfway through their initial analysis of the phone data. Adam noticed Marcus slumped in his chair, eyes closed. "Hey, brother, wake up."

Marcus opened his eyes. "Sorry, Adam. I'm running out of gas."

"Listen, you've got to see Mikey first thing in the morning. Why don't you head on home for a few hours? I'm going to finish up here pretty soon. The funeral is tomorrow at 10:00. I'll meet you at the cemetery, and we'll finish up this stuff afterward."

"You sure?" Marcus asked but was already out of his seat walking toward the conference room door.

"Get out of here. Go home to Makayla. I'll see you in the morning."

CHAPTER 11

MARCUS MANAGED A few hours of sleep before he got up, showered, and joined Makayla in the kitchen for coffee. They both treasured these moments they had together, especially when murder investigations required Marcus to be gone days at a time. Realizing the pressure and pitfalls police work could put on their marriage, they had agreed years before that Marcus would make every effort to not bring his work home with him. They left their house together at 7:00 a.m.—Makayla going to her job as manager of the West Ashley branch of BB&T Bank and Marcus going to his meeting with Mikey Brown. Marcus backed out of his drive and pulled up beside Officer James Rodriguez, who was stationed outside his house.

"Good morning, Rodriguez," Marcus said. "I'll be gone for the rest of the day, and my wife won't be back 'til mid-afternoon

She'll let you know when she's on her way back. Just make sure you're here when she gets back home."

"Will do, detective. You have a nice day."

~~~

The weather had turned overnight. A light rain was falling as Marcus waited at the entrance of the abandoned military hospital at the old Navy Shipyards. The deserted hospital, tucked along the Cooper River, was one of his favorite meeting spots. The navy facility began operations in 1901 and continued until 1996, when it was one of several military bases the Pentagon identified for immediate closure. Despite several attempts to revitalize the area, the hospital and most of the other buildings had been left virtually untouched for almost twenty-five years.

The hospital windows were boarded up, and the walls—inside and out—were covered with gang graffiti.

Marcus had been waiting there for a half hour. He irritably scrubbed the rain off his phone screen as he checked to see if he had missed a call from his Posse informant. Mikey was late. Ever since Adam had been shot by one of his snitches the previous year, the detectives had been especially cautious about how they set up meetings like this, and any irregularity tended to set off alarm bells. Still, he was very familiar with the deserted hospital. He favored using it because there were no security cameras and it was dead quiet—except for the periodic high-pitched sound of seagulls flying low over the desolate landscape.
~~~

He always made a practice of showing up early when meeting with informants—to secure the location and to make sure his snitch arrived alone. In his business, surprises could be deadly. He took another survey of his surroundings, which were shrouded in shadows as low-level dark clouds moved rapidly off the Atlantic, bringing the pungent salty scent of the ocean.

After an anxious fifteen-minute wait, he saw a lone figure rounding the far end of the building. He remained hidden until Mikey Brown reached the doorway. Marcus grabbed him and roughly pulled him inside.

"Did anyone follow you?"

"No," Mikey answered. "Who the hell's up this early anyway?"

"Did you tell anyone you were coming here?"

"Hell no! Why would I do that? I'd be in deep shit if anyone knew I was meeting a cop. I came straight from my place."

Marcus scanned the area again and, seeing no one, continued, "What did you find out about Joe Wallace?"

"Nothing. I mean no one's sad the guy went down, but I haven't heard anything about our people doing it."

"How about any talk that the Posse is hooking up again with Miguel Alvarez and the Sinaloa Cartel?"

"The only thing I know is that Spider's been meeting with someone from Mexico. And some of our guys are testing a new batch of smack on the street."

Marcus thought for a minute. "That new batch of heroin—do the bags have three skulls on them?"

"Yeah." Mikey smirked. "I ain't surprised your flatfoots took this long to figure that out."

"Don't be disrespectful, Mikey. And don't forget I can have my flatfoots make life miserable for you. Now, what about anyone putting a hit on my partner and me?"

"Nothing specific, but there's always talk about what you and your partner did to our business last year—not to mention that you put two of our toughest boys in the hospital. No one would cry if y'all went down either."

"Okay, go ahead and take off, but make sure you contact me if you hear anything."

Marcus stayed put for another few minutes until he saw Brown drive off in his Chevy Camaro—he was pleased that Brown knew enough not to have his system bumping.

Marcus headed to his car, parked behind an adjacent ruin. Just as he was about to unlock the door, a blow to the back of his neck dropped him to the concrete. He looked up to see two men standing over him—faces behind ski masks. Before he could even attempt to get up, a baseball bat smashed into him and broke several ribs—he heard them crack. Despite the pain, he managed to roll to his right, scramble to his feet, and tackle the bat man like the All-American linebacker he'd been in college. He got one punch in before his head exploded into a blinding flash of white light.

"*Suficiente! No me gusta la gente que me jode.*" Then the baseball bat connected to the back of his head, and his world went black.

Eventually, he became vaguely aware of the coppery taste of blood in his mouth. He managed to open one eye and saw nothing but the blurred image of an old man's face. He was cold, and the light hurt his eye. He tried to move his head but stopped when a lightning bolt of pain shot through him.

"You okay, fella?" The old man's voice sounded as if it came from deep within a tunnel.

It took a moment for the words to register before Marcus was finally able to mumble, "911." His head began to spin, and he felt himself falling until the blackness again consumed him.

~~~

The sky was overcast, the wet blacktop glistening as Adam drove through the ornate ebony gates of Holy Cross Cemetery. Seeing no other cars, he stopped at the office for directions to the gravesite. A dark-suited man gave him a map and identified the section and plot where Wallace's ashes were to be buried.

As he approached, he saw a black tent erected over the gravesite, a table underneath draped in dark-green cloth. No one was at the tent, but Adam did see a few cars parked on the blacktop alongside the grave. He jotted down the license plate numbers and waited in his car until a few minutes before 10:00 a.m., when another car pulled up. The man from the office got out and walked toward the tent. A moment later, Noah Buckley left his black BMW X6 M, followed by his wife and Elizabeth Wallace, each opening an umbrella before proceeding to the tent. Howard Jones and a few others, whom Adam assumed to be Wallace's colleagues, exited their vehicles and made their way toward the gravesite.
~~~

Adam left his Charger and glanced around and was surprised Marcus hadn't arrived yet. When he reached the small assemblage at the gravesite, he received curious stares from Noah Buckley and the lawyers.

The man from the office began talking about Wallace and his achievements. He mentioned some of the charities he'd supported, failing to note that most of the charitable donations were made by his law firm. The man's remarks lasted less than five minutes, after which he placed the urn into a cement vault. It would later be lowered the required three feet and covered with earth. No one else chose to offer remarks, and those in attendance were back at their cars less than ten minutes after the ceremony began.

As they walked off, Adam sidled up to Noah Buckley to ask when he and his wife would be available to meet again. "There are just a few more questions Detective Williams and I have for you and your wife."

"I understand, detective. If you'll give me a call tomorrow, we'll make time for you and your partner."

"I'll call you in the morning. Detective Williams and I would like to offer our condolences for your loss."

Noah Buckley smiled and said, "Of course you would."

Adam headed to Lockwood to continue analyzing the phone records and tried Marcus' cell on the way—it rang several times before going to message. A little concern began to creep in, but he knew Marcus could handle himself as well as anyone. Back at his desk, he continued the process of separating the phone numbers into two categories—seemingly routine, everyday conversations and outliers, the calls that may have been precipitated by specific events.

He called Marcus again with no luck and then phoned Makayla's cell. She answered with a hint of panic in her voice, the standard greeting from those with a loved one on the force.

"Adam?"

"Hi, Makayla. I was just wondering if you've heard from Marcus this morning?"

"No. We both left at 7:00, and I haven't talked to him since. Why?"

"No big thing," Adam said, not wanting to alarm her. "He was meeting someone this morning and hasn't showed up at the station yet."

"Who was he meeting? Do you think something's wrong?"

"No, I wouldn't worry. I'm sure he'll show up shortly. I'll let you know as soon as he does." He was beginning to sink and hoped that Makayla didn't hear it in his voice.

Shortly after he hung up, Merchant appeared in the bullpen and waved Adam into his office.

"What's up, Ed?"

"Sit down, Adam." Adam didn't obey, and Merchant continued. "Something's happened to Marcus."

"What the hell does that mean!"

Merchant sighed and closed his eyes for a second. "Marcus was found unconscious at the old shipyards. He'd been … beaten badly. That's all we know for now. He's at MUSC's Trauma Center." He reached into his desk drawer and pulled out his leather-encased captain's shield. "So, let's go. Get your keys."

"Shit, Makayla doesn't know. I need to call her."

Adam made the call—she seemed prepared for the worst when she answered. He told her Marcus was hurt, that he was at MUSC, but he didn't go into the extent of his injuries.

"How bad is it, Adam? You need to tell me."

"It's not good, babe, but I know he'll be all right. He's the toughest guy I know, and he's going to make it through this."

"I'm on my way," Makayla said, and the phone went dead.

Adam then called Tracy and asked her to go to Charleston Collegiate, pick up Piper, and take her to her house in James Island. He assured her he'd have Officer Fitzgerald there to meet them. This time, he couldn't conceal his anxiety, but Tracy didn't flinch—he couldn't imagine what he'd do without her.

On the way to the hospital, Merchant looked over at Adam. "What the hell was Marcus doing at the shipyards?"

Adam explained about his meeting with an informant to see if the Posse was involved in the Wallace murder. "The guy's name is Mikey Brown. He's been one of Marcus' snitches for years."

Less than five minutes later, Merchant and Adam were in front of the admitting attendant in the emergency room. Merchant read the attendant's nametag. "Ms. Hanson," he took a deep breath. "I'm Captain Merchant. We're here to see Detective Marcus Williams. Where is he?"

"Yes, sir. He got here about twenty minutes ago and was taken right back. Dr. Phillips is the attending physician." Ms. Hanson saw an ER nurse and called out, "Nancy, where's Dr. Phillips?"

"He's in the back," she replied.

Before the attendant could respond, Merchant said, "I'm Captain Merchant. Tell Dr. Phillips I need to speak to him immediately."

Ms. Hanson nodded her approval, and the nurse said, "Will do." She left through a door to the ER stations and reappeared a minute later with Dr. Phillips.

Merchant shook his hand. "Doctor, I'm Captain Merchant, and this is Detective Stone. I understand you're treating Detective Williams. What's his condition? Can we see him?"

"I'm afraid not, Captain. He's still unconscious. I only had time to make a cursory examination before he was taken upstairs. He has multiple contusions to the face and head and has sustained several broken bones. Our immediate concern is the possibility of internal bleeding. He's in surgery now. It'll be some time before we know his prognosis. You're welcome to wait outside surgery on the second floor."

"Thank you, doctor. We'll do that."

As soon as the doctor left, Merchant said, "I'll get back to the station and have vice track down this Mikey Brown character. Stay here and give me a call as soon as you hear anything about Marcus. I'm going to put another detective with you on the Wallace murder. I heard you got the phone and banking records. I'll also get you one of the techs to help with those."

Makayla got to the hospital twenty-five minutes later and was directed to the second-floor waiting room, where she met Adam. They hugged and, trying hard to keep it together, she asked, "Any word yet?"

"Not yet. He's in surgery now. They told me they'll let us know."

Makayla looked down the hall toward the operating rooms and whispered, "Damn you, Marcus. God damn you."

There was nothing more they could do but wait and hope for the best. Time dragged. When they weren't pacing, Makayla and Adam sat in dead-eyed stares, the awful thoughts in Adam's mind interrupted by regular update requests from Merchant and Taylor. There was nothing to tell them. Finally, at 3:00 p.m., a doctor appeared in blue scrubs, white surgical mask hanging loose around his neck.

Adam and Makayla quickly stood. The doctor shook Adam's hand and nodded to Makayla. "I'm Dr. DeCastro. Mr. Williams is out of surgery now and in the ICU. We have him sedated and will monitor him for the next hour or so. If he remains stable, he can be moved to a private room. You can see him then."

"He's okay?" Makayla asked, pleadingly.

"He will be." Dr. DeCastro pointed to his right forearm. "He had a displaced fracture of the right radius and ulna. He also had a broken right ankle, and two fingers on his left-hand sustained compound fractures. We've set all the bones and expect them to heal without any problems. There were a few broken ribs and multiple lacerations and bruises to his face and head—all of which have been addressed. He did have a serious concussion that caused a subdural hematoma, resulting in some pressure that built up in a portion of his brain. We relieved that pressure, and there should be no permanent damage. He may need some physical therapy, but other than that, he should recover completely."

The relief on Makayla's face was pronounced. She hugged the doctor and said, "Thank you. Thank you so much."

"You can wait here," DeCastro said, "and someone will let you know when he has been moved from the ICU and into a private room."

The doctor left, and Adam turned to Makayla with a smile. "I told you he's the toughest son of a bitch I know!"

Adam called Merchant to pass on the good news and told him that he was going to stay at the hospital until Marcus was settled in a private room.

"That's wonderful. When you get him settled, I want you back here at the station. We've got Brown sequestered in one of our interview rooms. We're going to wait until you get here to interrogate the little prick."

~~~

As hoped, Marcus was moved to a private room, and when Adam got back to Lockwood, he went directly to Merchant's office. "Where's Brown?"

"Room 1. He's been in there for about an hour and a half. Want me in there with you, or you wanna go solo?"

"I'll handle it."

Brown was slumped at the metal table when Adam entered. He locked the door and stared at Brown for a time without saying a word.
~~~

"Talk to me, Mikey Brown. What happened with you and Detective Williams this morning?"

"I don't know what you're talkin' about. Nobody's telling me shit about why my ass is here."

Adam walked over in front of the mirrored window and with his back to Brown mouthed, "Cut the video." He returned and moved behind Brown, putting both his hands on the back of the chair. "What happened with you and Detective Williams this morning?"

Mikey tried to stand, but Adam grabbed his shoulders and jammed him back down.

"I told you, I don't know what the hell you're talking about!"

Without warning, Adam pulled the chair backward and sent Brown tumbling to the cement floor. "Jesus Christ, man. What the hell do you want from me?" Adam put a boot on his chest.

"The truth, Mikey. Just the truth. I know you met Marcus this morning out at the shipyards. I also know he owns your ass. Now, get up and tell me what happened."

Brown stood. "All right. All right. So, yeah. I met him out there. He wanted to know if any of my boys smoked that Wallace guy. I told him no. He asked whether Alvarez was supplying us. I don't know anything about that, but maybe he is. And he wanted to know if any of us was planning on icing you guys. I don't know shit about that. Now can I get out of here?"

"You're not going anywhere until you tell me who took Marcus down after you set him up."

"What?" Genuine surprise registered on his face. "Wait a minute. What the hell you talkin' about?"

"Don't give me that shit. You know exactly what I'm talking about. Your buddies beat the hell out of Marcus. But I got bad news for you—he's still alive."

"Wait a minute! You sayin' someone took down Marcus? I don't know anything about that, man. You gotta believe me. He was cool when I left him."

Adam opened the door and called two officers into the room. He pulled a card out of his jacket pocket and started reading. "You have the right to remain silent. Anything you say can and will be used against you in a court of law …"

CHAPTER 12

ADAM WAS SITTING in Merchant's office alongside Chief Taylor. A silent fury swirled in the room.

"You didn't get anything from Brown?" Merchant asked.

"No, not really," Adam answered. "But I will."

"I hope so," Merchant said. He picked up his phone and punched in a number. "Gail, you can send in Officer Charles now." The door opened and Claire Charles entered.

"Adam, I put Claire on the Wallace case with you this morning. She's already been briefed on the investigation."

Two years ago, Claire Charles and her partner, Matt Manson—a duo inevitably referred to as simply "Charles Manson"—were the lead detectives on the murder investigation of Adam's wife.

Adam stood and shook her hand. She held on and said, "Adam, I'm sorry about Marcus. He helped me out when I joined the department fifteen years ago. He was a mentor to me, and I'll do everything I can to get the bastard that did this to him."

"Thanks, Claire, I know you will."

"Claire," Merchant said, "tell Adam what Billy Keefe told you."

"Wait a second, Ed," Adam interrupted. "Who the hell is Billy Keefe?"

"Tell him, Claire," Merchant repeated.

"He's the person who found Marcus. Keefe's an on-again, off-again homeless guy who hangs around the Navy Shipyards. When he's on the street, he sometimes stays in one of the abandoned buildings out there and said he slept there last night. The officers brought him into the station this morning. I interviewed him and, get this, he tells me he saw a short guy leave the old hospital building this morning and drive off. We figure that was Mikey Brown. A few minutes later, he said he saw 'a big black guy,' obviously Marcus, leave the building and walk to his car."

"You're telling me he saw the whole thing?"

"Apparently so. He said the black guy—Marcus—was parked in the lot next to a dumpster. Two men in masks came out from behind it. One of them had a baseball bat and nailed Marcus just as he was about to get in his car. They beat the hell out of him until a third man showed up and said something in Spanish. The other two guys stopped for a minute, and then the one with the bat hit Marcus one more time in the back of his head. After that, all three of them took off across the parking lot and disappeared."

"Was the third man wearing a mask?" Adam asked.

"I'm getting to that. Keefe said he was scared and hid in one of the abandoned buildings a long time after the three guys left. He finally went over to the parking lot where Marcus was and discovered his detective shield. I figure he was going through his pockets looking for money. He used Marcus' cell to call 911."

"The third man," Adam asked again. "Are you saying he did or didn't have a mask?"

"He didn't. So, when you were interrogating Mikey Brown, I was showing Keefe some mugs of Posse members. He didn't recognize any of them. Then Captain Merchant tells me about those letters you two got and gets me a photo of Miguel Alvarez."

"Shit," Adam said. "Tell me the guy recognized Alvarez!"

"You got it. He said Alvarez was definitely the third man!"

Taylor, who'd been quiet throughout, finally spoke. "Now that we know Alvarez is back in the States, we need to keep this to ourselves. I don't want him knowing we've ID-ed him. We also don't know whether the two other men came to the States with Alvarez. Those guys might have been Posse." Taylor turned toward Adam. "I get the feeling Alvarez isn't finished. From now on, I want an officer staying inside your houses 24/7 until we get him."

"Alvarez knows who I am and where I live," Adam said. "I've already arranged to move my daughter in with my mother-in-law. Fitzgerald has been covering my apartment. I'd like him to shift there and stay with them."

"You got it," Taylor said. "And get with your informants inside the Posse to see if you can get any intel on Alvarez's movements. Be clever about it, though—we can't have them knowing what we know about Alvarez. I'll have Simmons and Covell follow up on this with the FBI and DEA."

The meeting broke up, and Adam and Claire went to the bullpen. Adam explained to Claire what they had and how they were analyzing the data. Claire said she'd get the tech Merchant assigned, and they'd continue working on the records.

Adam left for the hospital. He wanted to be there when Marcus woke up.

~~~

The door to Marcus' room was open. It was quiet and dark inside, with the exception of continual beeps from the heart monitor and the flashing blue and red lights from the other equipment monitoring his vitals. Makayla was sitting next to his bed—eyes closed, a blanket around her shoulders.

Adam stood at the foot of the bed for a moment, surprised at how small Marcus looked under the covers, his face and head covered with bandages and his leg and arm encased in casts. After a moment, Makayla opened her eyes and whispered, "What time is it?"

"Almost 9:00 p.m. How's he doing?"
~~~

"He's just been sleeping. He's still sedated, but the doctor said he could wake up any time. The nurses brought me a ham sandwich and some ginger ale. They're over on the counter. I can't eat. You want them?"

"No thanks." Adam pulled up a chair to the other side of the bed. "I think I'll just sit for a while if that's all right with you."

"Of course," Makayla said with a small smile. "I keep telling Marcus he spends more time with you than he does with me. I think I'm jealous."

Adam returned the smile. "I know. Piper and Tracy say the same thing." They both were quiet after that—Makayla shutting her eyes again and Adam's gaze focused on his partner. After a while, he too nodded off.

He woke with a start. At first, he didn't know where he was and then saw Marcus in the hospital bed. He glanced at his watch—past 11:30. Makayla was still in her chair, but her eyes were open.

"You're up," she whispered.

"Yeah. What'd I miss?"

"You just slept through more sleep. He hasn't moved." She stood and gave a stretch. "I'll be right back. I need to use the restroom." Makayla leaned over and gave Marcus a soft kiss on his bandaged head. She whispered, "Love you, baby."

Makayla left the room, shutting the door quietly. Adam's eyes shifted back to Marcus just in time to see his eyelids flutter. He moved closer. "Hey, brother, it's Adam. You hear me?"

His eyes blinked a few times, and his head tilted toward Adam.

Adam touched his shoulder. "We're here, buddy. You're gonna be okay." He quickly went to the door, opened it, and saw Makayla halfway down the hallway. He called out, and she turned around. "He's awake!"

A moment later, they were on either side of his bed, Adam smiling and Makayla on the verge of tears. She bent down close and whispered, "It's me, baby." A faint smile appeared on his face, and he muttered something.

"I'll be right back," Adam said. He left and returned a moment later with two night nurses trailing him—one quickly checked his blood pressure, while the other adjusted the monitors and changed his IV.

Marcus' eyes were fully open now. "Water," he said, softly.

One of the nurses gave him ice chips and smiled at Makayla. "You can talk for a few minutes, but then he needs his rest."

Makayla smiled back and gently touched her husband's face. "Where am …"

"You're in the hospital, partner," Adam said. "Do you remember anything?"

"Three of them."

"Yeah, we know. Don't you worry."

"Sorry," he whispered, and his eyes closed.

"He needs to sleep now," the nurse reminded them.

~~~

Adam left the hospital and swung by Tracy's to check on Piper. Officer Fitzgerald was there and told him he'd be working with
~~~

another officer, so someone was always at the house. In less than a year, two gangs had come after both him and Marcus. No way in hell was he going to let them harm his family.

When he got back to the bullpen, it was deserted except for Claire Charles, who was at Marcus' desk with the murder book open in front of her. She heard Adam and looked up, bleary-eyed. "How is he?"

"He woke up and said a few words. Makayla's staying with him. He's gonna be all right." He glanced at the clock on the wall. "Why don't you take off and get something to eat?"

Claire smiled. "Not until I show you what we've got so far. Follow me." She headed for the conference room, where a tech was busy at work on his computer. He looked up at her when they walked in. "Adam, this is Steve Gagyi."

Steve looked like he could have been a college intern—all smiles, clearly excited about being part of the investigation. His enthusiasm made Adam feel even more exhausted.

"Okay," Claire continued. "We're not exactly sure what this means, so bear with me. I picked up this afternoon where you left off, analyzing the Wallaces' phone records. I found a whole bunch of calls to Joe Wallace from burner phones. I tracked a few of those to Chicago, and the rest were from here. You've got to assume the Charleston calls were from people like his bookie, his drug dealers, and some of the other shady characters he dealt with. And we know Chicago was all over him for his fifty-grand gambling debt."

"I'm with you so far," Adam said. "Go ahead."

"After I finished working his phone numbers, I started on his wife's. I didn't find anything out of the ordinary until I came across a call that was made to her from (708) 555-2456. The number turned out to be attached to a burner phone—the same burner number used for the calls made from Chicago to Joe Wallace. Obviously, we don't know who owned the phone and can't trace it to a specific location. However, it can be tracked to the first cell tower receiving the cell signal. In this case, the call was made from a burner phone located within a twelve-block radius of a cell tower located at 2131 South Halsted in Chicago's Southside."

"Wait," Adam said. "You're saying the same people who were calling Joe Wallace about his gambling debts called Elizabeth Wallace?"

"That's what it looks like," Claire said. "Now, the first call to Elizabeth was made about three weeks before her husband was murdered. As soon as the call was disconnected, she makes another call to (843) 555-8376. I looked it up, and that's a local Charleston number belonging to a Mr. Thomas Turner."

"Hold on a second!" Adam interrupted. "I interviewed Elizabeth Wallace yesterday, and a lawyer named Tom Turner with in there with her. Looks like we just got another player in the game."

"Right, but wait, there's more," Claire said, trying to keep her excitement in check. "A few weeks later, Elizabeth Wallace gets another call from the same Chicago burner phone. Just like before, she calls Tom Turner immediately afterward. The next day, she leaves for Nassau."

"Hang on a second," Adam said. "Let me see if I got this. Elizabeth receives a burner call from the same people in Chicago who are hounding Joe Wallace about his debts. Then she calls Turner. A few weeks later, she gets another call from the same people and talks to Turner again. Then she leaves for Nassau. This is getting interesting."

"And here's where it gets even more interesting. Steve, go ahead and tell Detective Stone what you've found."

"Sure. So, while Claire's working on Wallace's phone records, I'm looking at the banking information we got. I notice her father has been transferring $10,000 from his Wells Fargo account to her South State Bank checking account the first of each month. She uses some to pay bills, cashes some, and puts the rest into a savings account. You gotta figure this has been going on for a long time because the savings account had over $120,000. That is, until the day before she leaves on her trip. Records show there were two withdrawals from her savings account that day—one for $15,000 and another for $75,000. The $15,000 withdrawal was in the form of travelers checks, obviously for her trip. The $75,000 was taken out in cash."

"That's a hell of a lot of cash to take out of a bank all at once," Adam said.

"It sure is," Claire chimed in. "And banks have to report cash withdrawals like that to the IRS. But there's nothing that says you can't do it. It's your money."

"I hear you," Adam acknowledged. "So, Chicago might have called Elizabeth to get her to pay her husband's $50,000 gambling debt. It wouldn't be the first time she's had to fork over money for his debts. Maybe she called Turner to help her get the money to Chicago."

"If that's the case, why did Elizabeth withdraw $75,000 if Joe Wallace only owed $50,000?" Claire asked.

"Good question," Adam replied. "I'm afraid I don't have an answer for that—at least not yet. But what I do know is this Turner guy is somehow tied in with Nick Santoro."

"You mean Nick Santoro, as in the gambling, loansharking, prostitution, and money laundering rackets in Charleston?"

"That's him, and he's the nephew of Eddie Santoro, a big fish in the Chicago Outfit," Adam added.

"Wait a minute," Claire said. "If Elizabeth paid the fifty-grand her husband owed, why would Chicago want to kill him?"

"Exactly. They wouldn't," Adam said. "So, who does that leave that would benefit if Joe Wallace disappeared? The answer's pretty obvious: Noah Buckley!"

"So, what now?" Claire asked.

"This is the best lead we've got. Let's run with it. We definitely need to bring Noah Buckley, Elizabeth Wallace, and Tom Turner in for questioning." Adam looked at the clock. "Claire, you and Steve continue working the records. Maybe you'll find something else that ties Noah Buckley to the murder. I'll tell Merchant what we've got. I want to check on Marcus again, but I'll be back. That's some excellent detective work. Hell of a job—both of you!"

CHAPTER 13

ADAM WAS AT the Charleston County Detention Center at 8:00 a.m. the next morning. He'd arranged to follow up on Mikey Brown.

Brown had been deposited in a small room on the first floor. He was in green prison garb and looked like he hadn't slept, not unusual for a standard night in jail.

"Good morning, Mikey. Did they treat you good last night?" Brown was silent. "I've been thinking about what you said yesterday. You know, about not having anything to do with Detective Williams getting beat up."

"Aren't I supposed to have a lawyer when you're in here talkin' to me?"

"Sure, if you really want one. But all I want you to do is convince me you're telling the truth. Do a good job, Mikey, and I might be able to get your ass out of here. What'd you say?"

Brown went quiet for a minute, not sure if Stone was trying to set him up. "All right," he finally said, "I'll tell you. First off, do you really think I'm stupid enough to tell Spider Gomez I'm working with a cop? Christ man, I do that, and I'm a dead man walking. I've never even told my old lady about Williams. I went to the shipyards straight from my crib, and nobody fucking followed me. Like I said yesterday, when I left, Williams was just fine."

"If that's the case, Mikey, then who took down Marcus?"

Brown leaned forward. "I've been thinking about that, and I figure there must have been at least two or three guys took him down. No way is one dude going to do the job on Marcus. Anyway, whoever beat him was probably staking him out. I figure they followed him to the shipyards yesterday morning and decided it's a perfect place to pop him. And I can pretty much guarantee you it wasn't anyone from the Posse that did it. Don't make no sense coming after a cop when you're trying to setup distribution for a new batch of the black stuff."

"All right. I'm going to cut you loose. But if anyone asks where you were last night, you got shit-faced, the cops picked you up, and you slept it off in jail."

"I can do that."

"A couple more things. First, Marcus still owns your ass, and now I have a piece of it too. Second, we think Alvarez is in Charleston. You need to find out what you can on that and get back to me. I'd *really* like to know where he's staying. If you screw up and let them know we're looking, I'll send your ass right back here—or maybe worse. Do you understand?" Mikey nodded. "Don't nod, Mikey. I want to hear you say, 'Yes, Detective Stone, I understand.'"

Brown scowled and paused. But then he said it. "Yes, Detective Stone, I understand."

~~~

When Adam made it back to Lockwood, he found Claire and Steve Gagyi in the conference room they'd met in the night before.

Claire had already made separate calls to both Noah Buckley and Elizabeth Wallace requesting each come into the station to give formal statements. She'd emphasized it was standard procedure and wouldn't take more than a half hour or so. Both agreed, and she'd scheduled Buckley for 2:00 p.m. that afternoon and Elizabeth at 3:00 p.m.

Adam spent the next hour or so at the hospital with Marcus. Makayla had gone home to clean up and meet Officer Rodriguez, who would be shadowing her for the foreseeable future.

Marcus was awake and groggy from the pain medication, but he was able to communicate.

"How do you feel?" Adam asked, taking a seat next to the bed.
~~~

Marcus' head was almost completely bandaged. His jaw and eye were a dark shade of yellow-brown and badly swollen. "Been better. Hurts like hell," he mumbled.

Adam told him about Billy Keefe and how he identified Miguel Alvarez, the only one of his attackers without a mask.

"That son of a bitch," Marcus said. "Did you get him?"

"No, but we're working on it. Plus, we're making good progress on the Wallace murder too. Here's what we think happened." Adam went on to explain what they'd been able to glean from the phone and bank records. "It looks like Noah Buckley and maybe even Elizabeth Wallace are tied to the murder of Joe Wallace," Adam concluded.

Marcus' eyes were closed, and Adam thought he may have dozed off. But then he asked, "What about the Bloods?"

"We think the Bloods are out of the picture, and Spider Gomez and the Posse are looking less and less like suspects. It's now clear that Spider and the Posse are working with Alvarez to reestablish their Sinaloa distribution channel. It makes no sense for them to pull off a high-profile murder like this. That leaves us with Buckley and maybe his daughter as our probable suspects. But if Elizabeth actually did pay off her husband's fifty-grand gambling debt, then that leaves us with Noah Buckley as our prime suspect."

Marcus' eyes were still closed. Adam leaned closer. "Hey, buddy. You still with me?" Marcus didn't answer. Adam smiled and whispered, "Sleep well, my friend. Sleep well."

~~~
~~~

Adam wanted Claire Charles to join him in the Buckley and Wallace interrogations. He thought her disarming nature would go a long way toward easing whatever tension the interviewees brought into the room. Their plan was to have Adam begin in an entirely non-confrontational manner—to be almost apologetic for putting Buckley through a bothersome but necessary procedure. Hopefully, that would cajole him to become less guarded as the interview progressed, and when they saw that his defenses were down, Claire would begin to question him about possible dirt Joe Wallace might have had on his family. Adam would set him up, and Claire would take him down.

Buckley arrived right on time, and the desk sergeant ushered him into Interview Room 1. Adam found Claire, and they headed for the interview, not at all surprised when they opened the door and found an attorney seated alongside Buckley.

"Good afternoon, Mr. Buckley. Thank you for coming in today." He shook Buckley's hand and gestured toward Claire. "This is Detective Charles. You spoke to her earlier today, and she'll be joining us."

Buckley nodded and said, "Pleasure to meet you, detective. We'll also be joined by my attorney, Sam Mitchell." He turned to Adam. "Where's your partner? What was his name?"

"Marcus Williams. He's tied up with something and couldn't make it." Adam and Claire settled in—all smiles—and Adam got to it. "As I said, this won't take long at all. Just a formality. In cases like this, we need formal statements from people who were close to the victim." He sat a recorder on the table and noted the date, time, and location before identifying all parties present and shifting his attention to Buckley. "Mr. Buckley, Joseph Wallace was married to your daughter, Elizabeth Wallace. How long had you known your son-in-law?"

The interview continued with a series of benign questions about the Buckley family and its involvement in Charleston's business and political communities. Claire said nothing, likewise for the attorney, who nevertheless seemed on edge.

About twenty-five minutes in, Adam turned the questioning over to Claire. "Excuse me, Mr. Buckley. I understand your son-in-law had some, shall we say, troublesome social aspects to his life. He drank quite a bit and had some other habits that could be described as unsavory. Is that true, sir?"

"Well, I think—" Buckley started to comment but was interrupted by Mitchell.

"Hold it right there, detective. While Joe Wallace might have had some questionable habits, I don't see how his indiscretions have anything to do with my client. Mr. Buckley and his wife are well known and deeply respected here and throughout the state of South Carolina."

"I'm sure most everybody in Charleston society knows who your client is, Mr. Mitchell. It's just that I understand Mr. Wallace had accumulated a fair amount of gambling debts over the years, and Mr. Buckley and his daughter sometimes helped to pay off those debts."

"Joe may have gotten overextended a few times," Noah interjected, "and we did sometimes help ... remedy that. While we found Joe's gambling unseemly, he was family, and we had little choice."

"Of course," Claire responded, "family is an important thing. I was just wondering if you could tell us about how much money you provided to help Mr. Wallace when his finances got, as you say, 'overextended.' Just a ballpark amount."

"Noah, you don't have to answer that," Mitchell said.

"No, Sam. I don't have a problem with it." He directed his answer to Adam rather than Claire. "Most of the money Joe owed was gambling debt. He often came to me when he didn't have the money to cover his losses. A few times, he'd even ask Elizabeth for money, but most of the time I'd only have to give him a few thousand."

"I see," Adam said. "However, we understand that Mr. Wallace recently owed substantially more than a few thousand— more in the area of $50,000."

Mitchell again tried to intercede but was brushed aside by Buckley. "Your information is fairly accurate, detective. We eventually learned that the money I was funneling Joe wasn't going toward his gambling debts. This apparently had been going on for quite some time and resulted in his owing approximately the dollar amount you suggested."

"What happened when you learned the debt had reached such a level?"

Buckley paused for a second. "Before I tell you, I want to stress that at no time did my daughter or I do anything even remotely illegal."

"I understand," Adam said. "Please continue."

Mitchell suddenly stood and said, "I'm afraid this interview is over. Noah, I strongly recommend you don't say another word."

"Sit down, Sam!" Buckley said. Mitchell was upset at being rebuffed but returned to his seat and said nothing more. "As I was saying, my daughter and I never did anything illegal. When we did learn Joe owed his bookie $50,000, we kept it quiet for as long as possible. I didn't want Elizabeth involved in this and told her I would handle the situation. I suppose you could say this was the straw that broke the camel's back. Our family had been putting up with Joe and his pernicious ways for far too many years. We had merely been enablers—allowing him to take advantage of the family. I decided to no longer pay his debts, and when the people he owed the money to called me, I told them the family would no longer cover his gambling debts."

"When did you tell these people that you would no longer pay?" Adam asked.

"I don't remember exactly. I'd say perhaps about four weeks ago."

"I have one more question," Claire said. "We are aware that you transferred $10,000 to your daughter at the beginning of each month. This seems to have been going on for quite some time. Why did you do that?"

Buckley smiled. "So, you've gotten access to my bank accounts. I guess I'm not surprised. Let me just say this. Joe Wallace made a decent amount of money at Jones, Sanders, and

Cole, but he was a senior associate, not a partner. His paycheck normally should have covered his family expenses, but much of it was spent funding his personal escapades. I gave my daughter that money so she could pay bills and have enough left over to maintain a decent lifestyle. Don't forget, detective, I'm a father."

Adam checked his watch and saw it was approaching 3:00 p.m. "Mr. Buckley, we appreciate your candor. We'll let you go now but most likely will want to speak with you again."

"That would be fine, Detective Stone. We may not have liked Joe, but Shelly and I are willing to do what we can to help you find his killer."

Adam and Claire walked Mr. Buckley and his lawyer to the lobby. After they'd left the station, Adam said, "That was interesting. Now we know Chicago probably called Elizabeth to see if she'd pay."

"But remember, if she did pay the $50,000, why would they kill him?" Claire offered.

"Maybe they didn't," Adam answered, "but that's what we need to find out. Here's another thing. Like DA Stewart said, Joe Wallace probably had some dirt on the Buckley family, and that's why they put up with him for so long. Buckley must have known if he refused to pay, Wallace may go public with what he had."

"Sounds like a motive to me," Claire quickly replied. "Reputation is everything to these old southern families, and Noah Buckley certainly had the means to arrange for Wallace to disappear."

Adam agreed. "Listen, the desk sergeant just told me Mrs. Wallace and her attorney—I'm assuming it's Turner—are in

Room 2. I'm thinking we should postpone the interview until we get a better idea of Turner's involvement in this. I know we run the risk of Elizabeth and her father comparing their stories, but I still think it makes sense."

"Mr. Buckley seemed fairly open about what he'd done," Claire observed. "Remember, he didn't want his daughter involved, so maybe he won't let her in on what he told us. And based on what we learned, I'm not so sure we'll get the same type of cooperation from Mrs. Wallace."

"Right, I'll have one of the detectives tell them we were called out on a case and will need to reschedule. Let's get back to the conference room. I've got an idea."

CHAPTER 14

WHEN THEY GOT back to the conference room, Steve was still plugging away at the Wallaces' and Buckleys' phone and bank records.

"Steve, anything new?" Adam asked.

"Not really. This is a lot of information to track. Any ideas?"

"Actually, yes," Adam said. "Here's what I'm thinking. Based on the phone and bank records we've got, I think it's safe to say we've identified three prime suspects: Santoro and the Chicago mob, Noah Buckley, and Elizabeth Wallace. They've all got solid motives. We know they all talked, but the problem is we don't know what they said." Both Claire and Steve nodded their agreement.

"Now, we know Elizabeth took out $75,000 in cash. We assume part of that was probably used to pay off Joe Wallace's fifty-grand gambling debt." Claire and Steve again nodded.

"Now, if all that's correct, then how did the money get from Charleston to Chicago?"

"Exactly," Claire said. "Follow the money!"

A devious smile appeared on Adam's face. "And who did Elizabeth call each time right after she talked to Chicago?"

Claire took no time in responding, "Of course, Turner!"

"Right. Here's what I'm thinking. Turner is the probable link between Elizabeth and Santoro's Chicago Outfit. He also has ties to Nick Santoro here in Charleston. I figure Turner and Elizabeth Wallace have got to be talking. I say we put a Stingray on them and record their conversations. Maybe they'll let something slip."

Stingrays, also known as "cell site simulators" or "IMSI catchers," are surveillance devices that mimic a cellphone tower. They send out signals to trick cellphones into transmitting their locations and identifying information through the device rather than the closest cell tower. When the device is used to track a suspect's phone, it can be programed to selectively monitor and record individual conversations as well as text messages in real time.

"If we do that, Chief Taylor, or at least Merchant, will need to approve it," Claire said.

"You're right. So, let's go." The three of them went to Merchant's office and explained their plan.

"Interesting," Merchant said. "Before we do anything, I want the Chief's thoughts on this." He called Chief Taylor, and Taylor told them to come to his office and they'd talk.

After they'd settled in Taylor's office, Adam explained the rationale behind using a Stingray.

Taylor took a moment to consider it. "All right, based on what you told me, I agree this looks like your best option. However, I don't want this done to Noah Buckley or his daughter. Noah's influence with the powers-that-be could come back to bite the department. The lawyer, Turner, is another matter. I'll okay it for him, but you're going to need a warrant. If you can convince Judge Roberts to give you one, you've got a go from me. But you also need to bring District Attorney Stewart in on this."

"Thank you, Chief," Adam said. "We'll get right on it."

It took some time to write the warrant and affidavits. By the time they'd finished, it was past 5:00 p.m., and the judge had left the courthouse. Adam and Claire had to drive to Judge Roberts' residence in Mount Pleasant, and after several apologies, he reviewed and signed the warrant.

Back at Lockwood, the team gathered in the conference room to plan the next move.

"All right," Claire began, "how do you want to handle this?"

Adam looked at his watch. "Steve, how long will it take to set up the Stingray?"

"Once I have his cellphone number, it only takes a few minutes to program the unit."

"Perfect," Adam said. "We know Turner lives at the Mira Vista condos out on James Island. We'll call him from one of our blocked lines to make sure he's there. Assuming he is, Steve can set up the Stingray in the back of one of our unmarked vans. I'll get two officers to drive the van, and Steve can go with them and follow me and Claire out to Mira Vista. Once we all get there, make sure the van's parked in a location where you get good reception. Then Claire and I will go to his condo."

"What do we say once we get there?" Claire asked.

"He knows me from when I interviewed Elizabeth, and he wasn't too happy with the way I treated him—which is actually good. He'll be defensive. I'll introduce you, but you can just stay in the background. It'll give him something else to think about. I'll drop some hints about Joe Wallace's gambling debt and the $75,000. I might even ask him about Nick Santoro. All we want to do is shake him up a bit—get him thinking we know more than we actually do. I'll play it by ear. Hopefully, he gets nervous enough to call Elizabeth. Again, maybe he'll slip, and we'll get something."

It took about a half hour to get things set up. Adam had one of the female detectives make the call to Turner. He did answer, and then she apologized for calling the wrong number and hung up.

The detective nodded at Adam and he said, "It's a go!"

They were all out at Mira Vista and in position by a few minutes after 8:00 p.m. Adam knocked on Turner's door, and he answered dressed in a pair of jeans and a sweatshirt. He looked both surprised and confused. "Stone? What are you here for?"

He saw Claire. "Who's your girlfriend?" Claire remained standing against the wall by the door, her arms crossed.

"This is Detective Charles, and we have a few questions we'd like to ask you."

"And those questions, detective. What might they be concerning?"

Adam let that marinate a bit before answering, "May we come in?"

"No, you may not."

Claire stepped forward. "Perhaps Mr. Turner would like to come down to the station."

"All right, what's going on, Stone?"

Adam smiled and said, "Just a few quick questions, and we'll be out of your hair. Your choice: here or downtown."

"Jesus," Turner said, obviously pissed but trying hard to hide it. "Come in, but make it quick."

Adam and Claire entered his condo and got right to it. "How long have you known Elizabeth Wallace?" Adam asked.

"About six months or so. Why?"

Adam dismissed the question. "What about Mrs. Wallace's husband, Joe Wallace?"

Turner smiled. "What about him?"

"How long have you known Mr. Wallace?"

"Like most attorneys in Charleston, I knew Joe for years— as an acquaintance. I never knew him well. Again, why do you ask?"

"Just curious. How about Nick Santoro? Have you ever had the opportunity to represent him?"

Turner was clearly taken aback by the question, but he quickly recovered. "Now, detective, why would I want to represent Mr. Santoro? I've heard he has a somewhat dubious reputation."

"What can you tell us about the $75,000 Elizabeth Wallace withdrew from her bank?

Until that point, Turner had done a decent enough job masking his disdain, maintaining a somewhat dismissive attitude toward Adam's questions. But any hint of that now disappeared. After a short pause, he spurted, "I'm not sure I know what you're talking about. And even if I did, Mrs. Wallace is my client, and you know damn well our conversations are privileged."

Turner closed his eyes, conducting a little mental calculus to determine how much they knew. It couldn't be too much or they would have already arrested and charged him. He stood. "I think we're done here, detectives. If you have any more questions, you can talk to my attorney."

"That won't be necessary, Mr. Turner." Adam and Claire left without another word—leaving Turner wondering what just happened.

~~~

A few minutes later, Adam and Claire ducked into the back of the unmarked van with Steve at the controls of the Stingray. "Anything yet?" Adam asked.

"No, not yet."
~~~

"You really shook him up," Claire said, "I'll bet it won't be long before—"

And right on cue, Turner was making a call. It was answered on the third ring.

"For heaven's sake, Thomas. I told you not to call me."

"We've got a problem."

"What do you mean? What problem?"

"Detective Stone just stopped by my place."

"Why?"

"Listen, Elizabeth, we need to meet. Stone knows about the $75,000."

"What! How'd he find out about that?"

"I have no idea! You're home, right?"

"Of course."

"I'm coming over."

The call disconnected.

"God!" Claire said. "That was quick, and we've got it on tape!"

"Yeah, it's on tape, but think about it, Claire. The only thing they actually admitted to was something about $75,000. They didn't say what it was for or anything about a murder."

"Damn it, you're right." Claire was about to say something else when Turner's phone started ringing.

Adam held up his hand. "Hold on!"

"Elizabeth?"

"Don't you ever hang up on me again! What did they ask about Joe?"

"Not much. Stone just wanted to know how long I knew him. Look, I told you I'd take care of getting the money to Santoro. That's all. You set up everything else."

"Shut up, Tom! Listen to me. If they really knew about Joe, they wouldn't have let you go. Just keep your mouth shut. They can't prove anything."

"All right. Do you want me to come over?"

"No! I told you we can't be seen together until things settle down. Don't call me. I'll call you."

The call ended. Claire said, "Adam, it sounds like all Turner did was get the money to Santoro."

"You're right. Turner said he got the money to Santoro, but which Santoro, Nick or Eddie?"

"What's the difference whether the money went to Charleston or Chicago?" Claire asked.

"Come on, Claire. You're a detective," Adam said with a smile.

Claire immediately realized her mistake. "Right," she said, a bit of embarrassment showing. "If it goes to Chicago, we have to deal with our friendly FBI."

"Exactly," Adam replied. "But neither of them said anything about Joe Wallace being murdered. We still don't have an actual confession."

"We've got another problem," Claire said. "Elizabeth Wallace now knows we know about the money. She's got time to work up a story about it and make sure her story matches Turner's."

"That couldn't have been helped," Adam acknowledged. "I'll get ahold of the DA. It's her call what we do about it."

Adam called Elaine Stewart's cell. She was out having dinner with her husband and friends. He explained their meeting with Tom Turner that night and the recorded calls between Turner and Elizabeth Wallace. She instructed him to bring Turner into the station for questioning. "Keep him sequestered, and I'll be there as soon as I can."

Adam and Claire commandeered two officers and returned to Turner's condo.

He answered Adam's knock—his hair wet and a bath towel wrapped around his waist. "For Christ sake, Stone. What now? I told you I have nothing more to say to you."

Adam entered the condo, followed by Claire and the two uniforms. "Mr. Turner, I'm afraid you're going to have to come downtown. We have a few more questions for you."

"I'm not fucking going anywhere with you."

"Well, sir," Adam said, "as they say in the movies: we can do this the easy way or the hard way. Your choice." Adam nodded to the two officers, and they stepped forward.

Seeing he had little choice in the matter, Turner said, "At least let me put some damn clothes on."

The two officers followed Turner into his bedroom and watched as Turner angrily flung the wet towel onto his bed and put on respectable clothes. The officers then ushered him into the back seat of their patrol car. He was insolent all the way to the station and borderline seething when the officers left him in the interview room—Adam didn't think that was a bad thing at all.

"I have the right to call my attorney," a red-faced Turner demanded.

"Certainly," Adam said and pointed to the phone on the table.

Turner called a lawyer named Jack Morgan, took a seat at the table, and refused to say a thing.

"Make yourself comfortable, Tom. I'll be back shortly." He smiled and left the room.

Elaine Stewart called Adam thirty minutes later telling him she'd be there in about five minutes. Adam returned to the interview room, furtively turned on the recording app on his phone, and sat across from Turner.

"Can I get you some coffee or something?" Turner shook his head. "That's probably smart, Tom. The coffee here sucks. I'd get some donuts, but I'm trying to lose some weight. You know, Detective Charles and I have a bet. She thinks you know all about the $75,000. I bet her ten bucks you don't. What about it? Do I win the ten bucks?"

"Fuck you, Stone."

Adam just smiled and let the silence settle. He was practically reveling in it when the door opened, and Claire entered with Elaine Stewart.

"Detective Stone, what do you have for me?" Stewart asked.

"This is Thomas Turner. Tom, this is District Attorney Stewart, but I'm assuming you know who she is. She'd like to talk to you about Joe Wallace."

"I told you, I have nothing to say." There was defeat in his tone. His arrogance had slipped away.

"I see," Stewart said. "I'm sure Detective Stone has told you that we have some evidence that links you to a large amount of money that may be related to the murder of Joseph Wallace." The fact was that they weren't sure exactly *what* they had, if anything. But it was decided to embellish in an effort to pressure Turner. "I thought I'd give you an opportunity to explain yourself before I charge you."

"I told you I've got nothing to say."

"That is certainly your right, Mr. Turner. I understand you've contacted legal representation." She turned toward Adam. "Detective, I'll be with Captain Merchant. Please let me know when Mr. Turner's attorney arrives." She left the room without another glance at Turner.

"Tom," Adam said, "let me give you a piece of advice: don't piss off Stewart. We'll be back when your lawyer shows up." Adam and Claire left and went next door to the observation room, where they could watch Turner through the one-way mirror.

He sat at the table without moving, looking uncomfortable, almost certainly aware that he was being watched. After about five minutes, his foot began a nervous tap. "That jiggling leg tells me he's feeling the pressure," Claire said.

Twenty minutes later, Adam said, "Claire, go ahead and get Stewart. I want to be in the interview room before his lawyer gets there. I assume his attorney is going to be just as shady as his client."

Claire left and Adam entered the interview room. "Your lawyer just got here. I suggest you listen to the district attorney. You're running out of options."

A moment later, the door opened, and Morgan entered. "I'm Jack Morgan. I'll be representing Mr. Turner."

Adam nodded. "District Attorney Stewart should be here shortly."

A minute or two later, Stewart and Claire arrived. "Good evening, Jack," she said but made no effort to shake his hand.

"Has Mr. Turner been charged with anything?" Morgan asked.

"Not yet, counselor. I thought he might like to talk to us before we charge him in connection to the murder of Joseph Wallace."

"This is bullshit, Jack!" Turner said.

"Don't say another word, Tom," Morgan said in a calm voice. "My client hasn't done anything wrong. I suggest you either charge Mr. Turner or release him immediately."

Stewart said nothing for a few seconds and then fixed her gaze squarely on Turner. "Thomas Turner, you are being charged with murder in the first degree in the death of Joseph Wallace. Detective Stone, please have Mr. Turner taken to the detention center. I'll arrange for his arraignment." She turned back to Morgan. "Counselor, you can contact the court. They'll let you know when Mr. Turner is scheduled to appear. Have a nice day."

Stewart was about to open the door when Turner stood and called out, "Wait a minute!" She stopped and turned back. "I want to talk," he added.

"Tom, sit down and don't say another word," Morgan said.

"And what is it you'd like to talk about, Mr. Turner?" Stewart asked.

"Tom! I said be quiet!" Morgan again warned.

"I want to talk to my attorney in private."

"All right, Mr. Turner. We'll wait outside. Counselor, let me know when you're done."

She left, followed by Adam and Claire, who mouthed "holy shit" as she stepped into the hallway.

The three of them settled into the observation room, and Stewart said, "Looks like our strategy might be paying off. I'm not surprised—I know him, and he's not much of a lawyer, but he's smart enough to use his leverage."

"Do you think he'll flip on Elizabeth Wallace?" Claire asked.

Stewart smiled. "I guess we'll find out."

Turner and Morgan huddled together for almost ten minutes, and it was clear that Morgan wasn't happy with the conversation. Finally, he knocked on the door and told an officer they were ready.

Turner was looking at the ground, and a disgusted Morgan was looking at one of the stained ceiling tiles when the three filed back in. "Against my recommendation," Morgan finally said, "my client might be willing to talk to you."

"We're listening," Stewart said.

"If he does decide to talk," Morgan began, "he wants complete immunity."

Stewart smiled. "Now, Jack. You know that's not going to happen. What does he have?"

"Hypothetically," Morgan answered, "if Mr. Turner has information that indisputably connects Elizabeth Wallace to the murder of her husband, what would you be willing to do for us?"

"That obviously depends on what he has and if he's willing to stipulate to those facts in court."

"Hypothetically, if he can do that, he wants involuntary manslaughter, twelve to eighteen months."

"All right, here's what I'm willing to do," Stewart said. "If Mr. Turner was not physically involved in the murder of Joseph Wallace and can testify that Mrs. Wallace personally arranged the murder of her husband, he gets involuntary manslaughter, two to five. If he's a good boy, he'll be out in less than a year."

"Let me talk to my client," Morgan said. They huddled for a minute, and then Morgan said, "All right, involuntary man-slaughter, but make it one to three."

"I can live with that. Now, let's hear what Mr. Turner has to say."

"We're recording this," Adam said. "Mr. Turner will need to sign a transcribed copy of his confession."

Adam identified the date, time, and location. He continued, "I am Detective Adam Stone, and with me is Detective Claire Charles, Charleston County District Attorney Elaine Stewart, Mr. Thomas Turner, and his attorney, Mr. Jack Morgan. Mr. Turner, please tell us about your relationship with Mrs. Elizabeth Wallace and your knowledge relating to the death of Mr. Joseph Wallace."

Morgan nodded to Turner, and he began. "I met Elizabeth Wallace about six months ago during a Republican fundraiser at the Francis Marion Hotel." For the next thirty minutes, Turner described their immediate connection.

The day after the fundraiser, she reached out, ostensibly seeking his advice on a piece of commercial real estate she was considering. The real intention was clear, though. They met at a coffee shop but ended up at his condominium, where they had sex. Their relationship continued for the next several months, with her frequently complaining about her husband and his propensity for alcohol, drugs, and gambling. And while her re- vulsion for her husband grew, they were becoming infatuated with each other. They began talking about the possibility of marrying someday, but she told him Joe possessed damaging information that could destroy her family and that he would use it if she ever tried to leave him. But as the months went by, Joe's gambling losses grew worse, and her father kept giving him more and more money to pay off his debts.

Around then, she began to hint that their life would be so much better without her husband in the picture. Even though they kept their relationship quiet, Turner was becoming used to being around the money, power, and influence the Buckley family possessed. He couldn't help but visualize how his life would change as a member of her family. Finally, Elizabeth told Turner she had found some people who could make Joe go away and leave her family alone. All she needed was someone to handle the transfer of cash so she wouldn't be connected to the plan. She also told him she had planned to be out of the country when the people arranged for Joe's disappearance to further remove her from the situation.

"That's how I got involved with transferring the cash," Turner concluded.

"Excuse me, Mr. Turner," Stewart said. "To whom exactly did you give the $75,000?"

Tom Turner shut his eyes, vividly remembering the scene when Elizabeth told him when to deliver the money.

Elizabeth stood under the wood-beamed roof of the boathouse—her glass of scotch sitting next to a half-filled ashtray on the railing in front of her. High in the night sky, the moon's glow illuminated the slow-moving water as it slipped into Charleston Bay and on out into the Atlantic.

Some distance behind her, he was admiring the sleek lines of the silver and blue Sea Ray XLX 280 speedboat nestled in its metal lift.

He still stared at the Sea Ray and asked Elizabeth what she planned to do with the boat.

"I don't know. Probably sell it along with the rest of his toys."

Turner had never found Elizabeth's looks to be all that exceptional. Her face was beginning to show her age, but her body remained taught and shapely and she definitely knew how to use it. But he knew there were other assets she had to offer. He asked her if she had the money.

"It's over on the table by the chaise lounge," she replied.

He remembered the small Halliburton aluminum attaché case filled with banded stacks of $100 bills aligned neatly.

"When do you want me to deliver it?"

"I leave tomorrow at noon. You'll need to wait until I'm gone."

"When is the thing supposed to happen?"

"That's none of your concern, dear. Just do what I told you to do. Can you handle that?"

He snapped the case closed and sauntered over to where she stood. He slid his hands around the back of her Givenchy silk blouse and drew her close. "Of course, I can. I love handling everything you've got."

She gave him a peck on the cheek. "Good. Now go. I have to pack and get some rest. I'll call you from the island."

At this point, it became deathly clear to Turner that he was truly between a rock and a hard place. He was facing the possibility of being charged with murder or ratting on Nick Santoro—which could be a death sentence in itself.

Knowing he had no way out, he finally admitted, "I gave the money to someone who worked for Nick Santoro."

"And the name of that person?" Stewart asked.

He dropped his head. "Jerry Russo. I gave it to Russo."

"Thank you, Mr. Turner." She turned to Adam. "Detective Stone, I'll expect you and Detective Charles to follow up with me on Mr. Russo and Mr. Santoro."

"Absolutely," Adam replied.

"Mr. Turner, was Noah Buckley involved in any way with his daughter's plan to dispose of Joseph Wallace or the transfer of the $75,000?"

"No, I doubt it. Actually, she said she didn't want him to know anything about what we were doing."

Adam wanted clarification on a few points and a fuller picture of the events precipitating the transfer. After Turner satisfied those requests, Stewart had a final question. "Mr.

Turner, did you ever hear Elizabeth Wallace explicitly state that she had arranged for the murder of her husband?"

"She just said if I got the money to Russo, Joe would be out of our lives forever."

"That's it? And you didn't bother asking precisely what she meant by that?"

Turner thought for a moment, looking for a favorable spin. "Sometimes … she just took charge. I just did what she said. I just wanted to do my part and stay away from the rest."

"Excuse me," Morgan interrupted, "I think what my client means is that he was sure Mrs. Wallace wanted her husband out of the picture but not necessarily his murder. Isn't that correct, Tom?"

"Yes, that's what I meant."

Stewart directed her next comment to Jack Morgan. "I'm not here to talk about deals with a bullshitter. I want straight answers. No intelligent person in Turner's situation could have possibly thought he wasn't paying for a murder. And if this is all he has, his testimony isn't enough to convict Elizabeth Wallace. If your client wants a deal, he's going to have to wear a wire and get Mrs. Wallace to admit the $75,000 was payment for the murder of her husband."

"I can do that, Jack," Turner said, "but Elizabeth told me to avoid her for a while—until things settle down."

"All right," Adam spoke up, "can you think of any place she might go where she'd be alone? A place where you could approach her where she would be more apt to talk?"

"Well, there is one place that might work. After Joe was killed, she said she had to keep up appearances. She plans to visit Joe's grave every Saturday, to look like a grieving widow."

"I was at the funeral," Adam offered. "He's buried at Holy Cross on James Island. The place is huge. This could work. Turner could go early, wait until she arrives, and approach her at the grave. It sounds like our best shot."

"It might work," Stewart said. "Jack, we're going to keep your client at the detention center." She looked at Adam. "Detective Stone will be at the center Saturday morning to go over how the wire works and prep him." She turned her attention to Tom Turner. "If you make one false move or attempt to contact Mrs. Wallace in any way, the deal is off, and you'll be charged with murder. Do we understand each other?"

"Yes," Turner quickly answered.

"All right then. I think we're done here."

CHAPTER 15

MARCUS RECEIVED THE okay from Dr. DeCastro to be released on Saturday, and Makayla was at MUSC that morning to take him home. The swelling in his face and head had diminished somewhat, but it would still be some time before he was well enough to even think about going back to work.

It had been almost four days since Marcus was attacked, and aside from the occasional update, he was largely out of the loop on how the Wallace investigation was going. Knowing this, Adam called Marcus at the hospital at 7:30 a.m. Saturday morning to tell him what he'd learned from his follow-up meeting with Mikey Brown and what had transpired with the Wallace case and the lawyer Tom Turner.

"Sounds like you've been a busy boy, partner," Marcus said. "Anything new on Alvarez?"

"Not a whole lot. Our boy Mikey Brown told me the word is Spider Gomez has been meeting with someone from Mexico, and I gotta believe it's Alvarez. We now know that the three-skull heroin is being brought in by the cartel, and Alvarez is coordinating distribution through the Posse. Mikey said he'll let us know if he learns anything else—plus Merchant has Detectives Simmons and Covell turning over some rocks."

"I figured that much," Marcus said. "How are you going to handle that lawyer?"

Adam explained the potential plea agreement and how it largely hinged on whether wired-up Turner could get the goods from Elizabeth at the cemetery. "Claire and I will be out there with the techs listening when it goes down. We're working with DA Stewart on the whole thing, and if it works out like we hope, we can nail Elizabeth Wallace, Jerry Russo, and Nick Santoro for the murders of Joe Wallace and Tanya Scarcella."

"Sounds like the dominos are lined up," Marcus said with a smile.

"Right. Now all we need to do is get the first one to fall before the Feds think about sticking their noses into our case."

"Good luck with that."

~~~

Turner was wired and at the cemetery by 9:00 a.m. Saturday morning. He would wait until Elizabeth arrived and then approach her at the gravesite. Adam, Claire, and two techs were in range, housed in the back of a box truck with
~~~

Lowcountry Landscaping printed on its sides. Everything was set. Now the only question was whether Elizabeth Wallace would show.

Ten o'clock came and went. A good forty-five minutes passed without any sight of her. They were beginning to think the setup was a bust, but just then, Elizabeth's white Mercedes-Benz E-Class came rolling up. She got out with a small bouquet of flowers and placed them next to the grave, looking just as sad as can be—quite a performance, really.

After a few minutes, she glanced at her watch and started back to her car. She was about to open the door when Turner pulled in behind her and hopped out.

"Elizabeth, wait up, honey."

"What are you doing here?"

"Don't worry. Nobody followed me. We need to talk. I'm still worried."

"Damn it, Tom! Maybe they know about the money, but they don't know what it was for. If they did, we'd both be in jail. Now, just do what I told you to do. Keep your mouth shut and stay away from me."

"But what happens if they find out? I had nothing to do with having Joe killed."

"No, Tom, that's where you're wrong. It doesn't make any difference that I arranged for the money for Santoro to kill Joe. You delivered it, and that makes you just as guilty for his death as I am. So do exactly what I said and keep your mouth shut. They won't be able to prove anything. I'm leaving now, and don't call or come near me until I tell you it's all right."

Adam and Claire looked at each other, huge smiles spreading across their faces. "We got her, Adam. We got the bitch!"

Adam turned to the techs. "Did you get that?"

"Got it!"

Adam yelled to the driver of the truck, "Go!"

Just as Elizabeth settled into her Benz, they had the nose of their truck against her front bumper. And as they popped out, a squad car sidled up against her passenger door, fully boxing her in.

Elizabeth Wallace sat stunned behind the steering wheel. An officer yanked open her driver's side door and yelled, "Get out! Get out now!"

The second Elizabeth was out of the car, the officer grabbed her, spun her around, and pushed her onto the hood of the car. He cuffed her and stood her back up.

By that time, Adam and Claire were directly in front of her.

"Go ahead, Detective Stone," Claire said. "Do the honors."

Adam stepped forward. "Mrs. Elizabeth Wallace, you are under arrest for the murder of Joseph Wallace. You have the right to remain silent. Anything you say can and will be used against you in a court of law…"

When Adam finished reading Elizabeth her Miranda rights, she turned and stared at Turner. She still had a confused look on her face when Turner opened his jacket and showed her the wire. She shook her head and mumbled, "You stupid son of a bitch."

Adam smiled at Turner and said, "Good job." He smiled back, but the smile quickly disappeared when Adam reached behind him and pulled out his handcuffs. "Turn around and put your hands behind your back."

The officers had Elizabeth in the back of one squad car and Turner in another heading back to the station. Claire and Adam were walking back to the truck when she playfully punched him on his arm and said, "God damn it, Adam. We did it."

Adam responded with a less than enthusiastic, "Yeah."

Claire heard the joyless tone in his voice. "What is it?"

"Sorry, Claire. You're right. We got her, but we're not finished. We know Russo got the money, but that doesn't mean he killed Wallace—or even prove that Nick Santoro ordered the hit. He's got lawyers that know every trick in the book. Plus, nobody's talking about poor Tanya Scarcella. Collateral damage is a hell of a way to describe the end of someone's life. Marcus is all busted up, and I've got police officers living with my family."

"I understand," Claire said. "Listen to me, you're one of the best detectives I've ever worked with. I know this thing isn't finished, but we'll get it done. I promise you that!"

~~~

The officers transporting Elizabeth Wallace called ahead to advise Chief Taylor and Captain Merchant she had confessed to setting up the murder and they were on their way back to the station. About fifteen minutes later, the truck Adam and Claire were in pulled in and parked behind the squad cars at the rear of the station.
~~~

Adam and Claire hopped out of the back of the truck and instructed officers to take Turner into the station and arrange for his transport to the detention center. Merchant was there to meet them and said, "I hear you got Wallace. Now follow me inside and get started on the paperwork."

Both Adam and Claire were a bit surprised with the less than enthusiastic reception they received from Captain Merchant— not exactly what they were expecting having just solved a major murder investigation. Claire shrugged, and they followed Merchant inside. As they turned the corner and walked into the bullpen, they were met by a smiling Chief Taylor and a room full of detectives and uniformed officers who broke into a round of applause and cheers.

Merchant turned around with a huge smile. "Nice collar, detectives!"

Taylor shook their hands. "Well done, you two."

"Thanks, Chief," Claire said, "but I'm just filling in for Marcus. This one's his collar."

"I think we can find three collars somewhere around here!" the chief replied. "Seriously, that was some excellent detective work."

Claire looked at Adam. "Thank you, sir. But we're not finished. We've got more work to do."

"Chief, do you mind if I take off for an hour or two?" Adam asked. "I'd like to tell Marcus in person."

"Go ahead. I'm sure the paperwork can wait a few hours."

~~~
~~~

Makayla answered the door when Adam knocked. She had taken the week off to stay home with Marcus. "Adam, this is a nice surprise. Come on in. Marcus is resting in the family room."

Marcus, in his pajamas and bathrobe, was fully extended in a recliner. He was coming along, but it still looked like he'd just had his ass kicked.

"Hey, partner. Why aren't you out there catching the bad guys?"

"Marcus, you're looking better. I see Makayla's taking good care of you."

"She always does. How's the Wallace investigation going?"

"Oh, you mean the Joe Wallace murder case. I'm not working on that one anymore."

"What do you mean you're not working on it?" A huge smile spread across Adam's face, but he said nothing. "Wait a minute," Marcus said and tilted himself up, grimacing a bit as he did. "Shit, man. Are you telling me you solved the son of a bitch?"

"No, Marcus. I'm saying *we* solved the son of a bitch!"

Adam took the next ten minutes explaining how the whole thing went down and what still needed to be done. "We still need to find out who actually killed Joe Wallace and Tanya Scarcella. So, get your ass healthy, and we can finish what we started."

"Oh, man. I wish I could have been there—and I could have been. I'm certainly in decent enough shape to sit in the back of a damn box truck, but listen, thank Detective Charles for me. What's the latest on Alvarez?"

"Nothing, really. We know he's here, but Chief wants to keep it quiet. We don't want to spook him. Hopefully, we'll get a break soon. Anyway, I need to get back downtown and start to push some paper. Like I said, you need to rest and get your ass back to work. They're going to take Claire away from me, and I'm going to get lonely." Adam put his hand on Marcus' shoulder. "Seriously, everyone wants you back. I'll catch you later, brother."

CHAPTER 16

WHEN ADAM GOT back to Lockwood, he was told to go straight to Taylor's office. As he walked in, Captain Merchant, Claire, and Detectives Simmons and Covell were also there. No one was smiling.

Chief Taylor pointed at the only empty chair. "Adam, take a seat." Adam sat and the chief continued. "You all did a great job so far on the Wallace murder, but there's no time to sit and celebrate. You've got Russo and Santoro to deal with, but something else just came up. I spoke with Terry Blackwood about an hour ago. He's picked up some rumblings that something big is about to go down with Miguel Alvarez and Spider Gomez. We know the Posse has been testing the three-skull heroin on the street, and the street apparently loves it."

Adam wasn't surprised. A meeting between Alvarez and Spider Gomez to finalize their transaction was imminent. But he knew Alvarez had to act quickly—the longer he remained in the States, the greater the chance he'd be apprehended. Since his escape back to Mexico a year ago, he'd become one of the FBI's most wanted fugitives. Adam was stunned he'd even attempted, much less succeeded, in making it back to the States. As Merchant had pointed out, the fact that Alvarez was personally coordinating the Sinaloa Cartel's reconnection with the Posse was most likely his way of rebuilding his reputation within the cartel. It also gave him the opportunity to seek revenge against Marcus and Adam for their part in discovering and aborting his last attempt.

It was Captain Merchant who spoke next. "We're running out of time if we're to have any chance of stopping this new type of heroin from getting a foothold in Charleston. Blackwood thinks a major shipment of product has already arrived in Charleston. Word is it came in on a cabin cruiser bypassing any detection by the Coast Guard or DEA."

"Right," Chief Taylor said. "The strange thing is he picked up his intel from one of the Bloods. The meeting's supposed to happen in the next day or two—maybe even tonight. He doesn't know for sure where it'll be, but we know the Posse runs a small auto salvage business out in Goose Creek. Spider has used that spot before. Apparently, it's out in the country, nothing much around it."

"I've advised our SWAT Team commander, Chico Walker," Merchant confirmed, "and he's already put a plan in motion, one that will be operational asap in case the meeting goes down tonight."

~~~

SWAT, DEA, and FBI agents were assembled at Lockwood at 6:30 p.m. that evening. The Posse's preferred hangout was at a downtown bar called the Coach House. Undercovers were stationed there and outside Spider's apartment on Nassau Street. A third undercover was out in the Goose Creek woods, keeping an eye on the salvage yard.

If Gomez was observed driving east on I-26, it would be assumed the meeting was on and would be held at the Auto Salvage location. The SWAT Team, along with FBI and DEA agents, would then be deployed to that location. Once Chico Walker's SWAT Team arrived, he would assess the situation and initiate the assault.

Adam felt good about the plan, aside from a significant drawback: Merchant said that he and Claire could come along but had to stay out of the action—the case belonged to Simmons and Covell now.

Adam wasn't very good at watching from the sidelines, though. He had a few ideas of how he might play the game.
~~~

CHAPTER 17

ADAM RECOUNTED TO Claire Marcus' interrogation of Carlos Santana and the subsequent visit to his Midland Park house. He also told her that Santana was both the bodyguard and driver for Spider Gomez.

"I think I know where you're going with this."

"Chances are if the meeting with Alvarez actually takes place, it'll probably be at that Goose Creek salvage yard. But no matter where it happens, you know Carlos Santana will be driving Spider there and sticking around to protect him."

Claire smiled. "Detective Stone, how would you feel about spending the night with me in a car watching Mr. Santana's house and maybe even following him if he decides to take a ride?"

"I think that's an excellent idea."

~~~

As day gave way to dusk, Adam and Claire were parked around the corner from Carlos Santana's Midland Park cul-de-sac. The vantage, behind a row of hedges, provided both cover and a decent view of Santana's home, which sat dark, no pit bull roaming in the pen.

Adam unscrewed his thermos and passed it to Claire. "Coffee, detective?"

"Thanks. I get the feeling it won't be the last cup we drink tonight."

A few hours later, a late-model black Nissan Altima pulled into the drive. Santana got out and entered his house. Ten minutes passed before he reappeared, got back in the Altima, and left. They watched him pass, and then Adam hit the ignition and eased along behind him.

They trailed at a safe distance as Santana entered the ramp onto 26 toward downtown Charleston. He exited downtown and pulled up in front of Spider Gomez's Nassau Street apartment. A minute later, Spider and another man, briefcase in hand, got into the Altima. Things were progressing as expected—until Santana took the Crosstown to 17 rather than getting back on 26.

"Where the hell are they going?" Claire asked.

"I don't know, but it sure isn't Goose Creek."

He got Merchant on the phone and provided the update—the response wasn't what he expected either.
~~~

"You must be mistaken, Adam. Our undercovers saw Gomez and two of his men leave the Coach House Bar about a half hour ago. They're in a Cadillac Escalade heading toward the salvage yard. We're a few minutes away. Seems like that meeting with Alvarez is on."

"Ed, I don't know what to tell you other than Claire and I definitely saw Spider leave his apartment and get into a Nissan Altima with Carlos Santana."

"If what you say is true," Merchant said, "one of us got played. Listen, stay with whoever you're following. We're going to move on the building. Let me know what happens on your end."

"Will do," Adam said and disconnected the call. "Why don't you call us in backup, Claire. For now, we're on our own."

"Got it," Claire replied and made the call.

After following the Altima for a while, it suddenly picked up speed, and Adam pushed his Charger to keep up. A few minutes later, the Altima turned left off 17 and parked behind an abandoned gas station at the corner of Amarillo Road and 17. Adam kept driving for another quarter mile then made the turnaround and headed back toward Amarillo. He shut off the lights and pulled off to the side well before the gas station.

"What now?" Claire asked.

"Let me think. We know Spider thought he'd be under surveillance, so he's on the lookout. Merchant bought it, and now he's in Goose Creek. Our backup is almost thirty minutes away, and it seems like Spider and Alvarez are about to rendez-vous right in front of us."

Adam paused for a moment, looking off toward the dark gas station. "I'm going to go see what's going on up there. Go ahead and call Merchant and tell him what's up and where we are. I don't know whose jurisdiction we're in but find out and call them. Once I get a look, I'll come back."

"Okay, be careful and get back here as soon as you find out who's in that building."

Adam checked his Glock and slid from the Charger. He jumped a roadside ditch and made his way to the rear of the gas station through a wooded area, hoping that the highway whir was loud enough to mask the crack of sticks breaking underfoot. Three cars, including the Altima, were parked behind the building. He scanned for presence outside; not seeing any, he slunk his way alongside a grimy window. He eased himself up and saw a table illuminated by the glow of cellphone flashlights—an open briefcase sat beside several large taped bags of what must have been heroin.

Spider Gomez, Carlos Santana, and another man were on one side of the table. Miguel Alvarez was on the other side, flanked by another man he didn't recognize. They were engaged in an animated conversation, but Adam couldn't hear a word.

Adam turned to go back to the car but froze when his cellphone rang. "Shit," he whispered, quickly killing the call. He held his breath and didn't move. Suddenly, he heard the click of a trigger being engaged and felt the cold steel barrel of a gun against his temple.

"*Que acaba de cometer mal error, idiota.*" He felt the Glock being removed from his holster. Then a vicious blow knocked him unconscious.

Stone was dragged into the garage, and Spider ordered one of his men to check the outside of the station. The man returned a moment later. "Don't see nobody else. Quiet out there."

Spider was obviously nervous. "Let's finish this!"

At some point, Adam's eyes began to focus, and he saw the face of Miguel Alvarez staring at him. "You are a fool, Detective Stone. And now you will pay for your foolishness." Alvarez backed away. "I'm going to take a piss. Javier, kill the gringo."

Adam was still dazed but realized that he was seated in a chair with his hands tightly secured behind him. His head throbbed, and he could taste blood. A large man removed a knife from his belt and walked behind him. He felt his hair being grabbed and his head pulled back. He shut his eyes, visualized the face of his dead wife and smiled. If he was about to die, he wanted Ann with him.

At that instant, he heard a loud *crack* and felt something wet hit the back of his neck and head. A second later, the room exploded in gunfire. Adam tucked his chin to his chest while the bullets cracked and echoed. Then, as quickly as it began, the shooting stopped. He opened his eyes and saw five men—two with sawed-off shotguns and the others with handguns, all with stockings pulled over their faces. One man grabbed the briefcase, and the others began stuffing the kilos of heroin into a canvas bag.

"Let's get the fuck out of here!" one shouted. Another stopped in front of Adam—he was smiling underneath the stocking. "Relax, white boy. Today ain't your day to die. You my message man. Tell everyone this one's for our brother, Demarco Moore." He was gone a second later.

The room was filled with smoke and the pungent stench of nitroglycerin. Adam felt numb sitting there, tied up, trying to make sense of what had just happened. It was the Bloods. He was appreciating the irony of the situation when he heard a noise. He looked to his left and saw Miguel Alvarez appear from behind a counter where he'd been hiding. He stood, taking in the death around him.

He saw Adam still tied to the chair and walked toward him, picking up a handgun from a dead man on his way. He didn't speak until he was right in Adam's face. "Are you a religious man, Stone?" Adam said nothing. Then Alvarez took a step back and pointed the gun at Adam's face. Adam refused to shut his eyes or turn away. "Now is the time to say a prayer," Alvarez said, his voice filled with loathing.

Adam always knew there was a chance he might be killed in the line of duty. He'd resolved that the time was now. Then he heard a gunshot and saw Alvarez's head snap back as a bullet dug into the center of his forehead. He spun his head around and saw Claire Charles crouching on a knee next to the side door, her Sig Sauer extended in front of her.

She quickly moved forward with her gun trained on Alvarez, a halo of blood expanding from his head. She placed two fingers on his neck, felt nothing, and turned to face Adam.

She pulled a knife from her ankle sheath and cut the rope that held his hands.

"Good to see a friendly face," he said shakily.

Adrenaline still pumping through her body, she simply said, "Let's get you the hell out of here."

She was helping Adam up when headlights from two squad cars flooded the station with white light. A moment later, one of the officers helped Claire get Adam out of the station. Minutes later, several more police cars arrived at the scene.

"What the hell happened in there, Adam?"

He tried the best he could to piece together what happened. He finished by saying, "The Bloods took out everyone in there except for Alvarez. I remember him ordering one of his men to kill me and then he left. He must have gotten out in time to hide right before the Bloods hit the place."

"I'm sure you're right," Claire said. "I was in the car on the phone with Merchant when an SUV turned off the highway and parked a few hundred feet to the other side of the intersection. That's when I saw four or five men get out and disappear into the woods. By that time, you'd been gone too long, and I thought something might have happened to you. I left the car and was about halfway to the garage when I heard the shooting start from inside the station. I hit the ground, but the gunfire stopped almost immediately. A moment later, I saw the men running out of the building. They all got in the SUV and took off, but it was too dark to get the plate number. I ran to the window on the side of the building just in time to see Miguel Alvarez in front of you holding a gun. I barely had enough time to get inside and take the shot."

"Your timing was perfect," Adam admitted. "Another second or two and I'd been history. What happened with Merchant and everyone else?"

"He called right after you left and said when they got to the Auto Salvage place, he realized he'd taken the bait and followed the decoy. The guys in the Escalade were there, but no Spider, Alvarez, drugs, or money. I was in the middle of explaining where we were and what was happening when the SUV with the Bloods showed up."

Over the next hour, more officers and detectives arrived along with an EMS van. Adam and Claire were giving their statement to one of the detectives when Ed Merchant arrived.

He got out of his car and jogged over to Claire and Adam. "Christ, I'm sorry!" He noticed the bandage on the back of Adam's head. "We need to get you to the hospital."

"No. I'm fine, Ed. All I want to do is go home and see my daughter. I'll give my formal statement at the station tomorrow."

"That goes for me, too," Claire quickly added.

"Adam, I'll have an officer drive you home. Give me the keys to your car, and I'll have another officer drop it off at your apartment." He turned to Claire. "Detective Charles, I'll need your weapon and shield. You're going to have to go to the station for a blood test and be placed on paid administrative leave until the deadly force investigation is completed. I'm sorry, Claire, but that's the way it's got to be."

"I understand." Claire removed her Sig Sauer, and it was put in an evidence bag. "Adam, I'll see you at the station tomorrow."

She started to walk away, but Adam called after her. "Wait a minute, Claire." He got up and pulled her close. He whispered, "You saved my life tonight, partner. I'll never forget that."

~~~

It was well after 3:00 a.m. by the time Adam was dropped off at Tracy's house. Officer Fitzgerald let him in, and he went straight to Piper's room. She was fast asleep. He sat on the side of her bed for a time, just watching her sleep. Finally, he bent down, kissed her forehead, and whispered, "I'm home, sweetheart. I'm home."
~~~

CHAPTER 18

ADAM OPENED HIS eyes and squinted against the morning light streaming through the living room window. It took a second for his mind to register where he was, and then he felt a dull ache in the back of his head. He heard Tracy in the kitchen and managed to stand up and make his way there.

"Good Lord, Adam," she said. "What in the world happened to you last night? I was up early and found you asleep on the couch and had to fight the urge to redress that bandage on your head. Come here and let me look at you."

"Oh, I'm fine. This is nothing." He slumped into a seat at the kitchen table. "Where's Piper?"

"She's still sleeping, dear. Now, for heaven's sake, tell me what happened."

"Things got a little rough, but the folks who are responsible for it have been brought to justice. I can't promise there won't be more danger in the future as long as I have this job, but I think we can sleep a little easier tonight, which is worth a knock or two on the head."

"Do you think it's safe enough for Piper to go back to the apartment?"

"I know how hard this has been for you two, but I want Officer Fitzgerald to stay here with you two for a little longer."

Adam had just finished when he heard, "Good morning, Daddy." Pajama-clad Piper was smiling at him from the doorway.

"Come here, sweetheart," he said and gave her a big hug.

After breakfast, Adam cleaned up and drove to Marcus' house, where he recounted the succession of events that led to the Bloods' raid at the abandoned gas station, the death of Spider Gomez, and how Claire had saved his life by taking out Miguel Alvarez. Marcus couldn't get enough details. He asked question after question, each answer inspiring another question, until Adam needed to leave and get down to Lockwood to give his statement.

At the door, Adam turned back and said, "Looks like I'm going to be all by my lonesome until Claire's deadly force investigation gets wrapped. I need you to get your ass better. How long do the doctors say it'll be before we get you back to work?"

"I'm working on it. They tell me I'll need some physical therapy as soon as I get these casts off, but man, I'm feeling good." Marcus hopped up and grabbed his crutches to display a little alacrity. "See what I'm saying? But listen to me, brother. Don't you go finding another partner while I'm getting better!"

"Not a chance, my friend. Not a chance."

~~~

Although her reinstatement was never in question, it took more than a month for Claire's deadly force investigation to make its way through the necessary protocols.

The day after the investigation was completed, Merchant had Claire in his office for an informal reinstatement ceremony. Chief Taylor, Matt Manson, and Adam were there in support when Merchant slid her handgun and shield across his desk to her.

Claire smiled and picked them up. "Thank you, sir."

"No, detective," Merchant said, "it's everyone in this department who owes *you* a thank-you for your exemplary service. I'm reassigning you to Matt Manson." He smiled. "We've all been waiting for Charles Manson to return to the force."

Claire shook the Captain's hand and beamed.

"Oh, and there's one more thing," Merchant said. "Detective Stone, as you don't have a partner now, I'm assigning you a detective-in-training. This fellow is a bit wet behind the ears, but I'm sure you can straighten him out."

Adam was obviously disappointed. "How long is this going to last, Ed?"
~~~

Merchant stood and said, "It's going to last as long as it takes for you to show this young fellow the ropes, detective. As a matter of fact, your new partner just walked into my office."

Adam turned around. Standing in the doorway was Marcus Williams. "Hey there, partner," Marcus said. "Are you ready to go catch some bad guys?"

A huge smile spread across Adam's face. "Sure…as long as you remind me how it's done, partner."

THE SANDMAN

CHAPTER ONE

DETECTIVES ADAM STONE and Marcus Williams joined many of their fellow police officers, local politicians, and assorted dignitaries at City Hall for Ed Merchant's swearing in ceremony as Charleston's new chief of police. Merchant had been a captain on the force for the past eight years and was replacing Dan Taylor, the outgoing chief and a true icon in South Carolina law enforcement. The appointment surprised no one, as there was never any doubt that Merchant would be the new chief once Taylor decided to retire.

Chief Taylor's career spanned some forty years—the last twenty-two as chief. Marcus joined the department the same year Taylor became chief, and Adam became a member of the force a few years later. The detectives had been partners the last eight years and were part of Captain Merchant's Special Operations Unit.

Ed Merchant's promotion to Chief left the vacancy for the position of captain and required Mayor John Tecklenburg to appoint a successor. To the surprise and disappointment of many officers in the department, Tecklenburg appointed Lieutenant Frank Boyer to fill the captain position. Boyer had transferred in from Chicago as a lieutenant on Charleston's force only three short years ago. The disappointment was not only because of his short tenure with the department but also due to a personality that was viewed as arrogant and egotistical. It was obvious his appointment was based on politics rather than competence. Even though Boyer was a lieutenant in the department, Adam and Marcus had little if any interface with him. As members of the Special Operations Unit, they reported directly to Captain Merchant.

Marcus leaned into Adam and lowered his voice, "Looks like Boyer's our new boss. If being an asshole was a crime, Frank would be serving multiple life sentences. This should be fun."

"Fun might not be the right word, my friend," Adam responded. "Let's just keep our heads down and see how long he lasts."

Like most any organization, the department had its share of boot lickers and ass kissers that would suck up to their superiors no matter how inept and autocratic they were. Adam and Marcus would take their orders as given but had been professionals too long to play those games. There was no doubt in anyone's mind that both Adam Stone and Marcus Williams could have been in line for the captain's job had they not passed on promotions in order to remain on the front lines. Neither of them had the inclination to leave the street. Their tandem work had consistently led the department in the number of closed cases for the past eight years. Their relationship had grown well beyond that of being merely partners. They'd become best of friends.

Their backgrounds could not have been more different. Adam was raised in the predominately white, upper middle-class Charleston suburb of Mt. Pleasant, and Marcus in North Charleston's gang-infested Union Heights neighborhood. Marcus spent much of his youth in the gang culture up until his freshman year at North Charleston High School. His unusual size and physique for his age caught the eye of the high school's head football coach. Had it not been for the coach convincing him to come out for the football team, he would have most likely ended up as a gangbanger. By his senior year in high school, he was 6' 4' and 260 pounds and had earned first-team All-State honors and a full ride football scholarship to Clemson University. Marcus' accolades on the gridiron did not stop there. During his final year in college he was named a second-team All-American linebacker. He was even more proud when he learned of his selection as a member of the Academic All-American Team his senior year at Clemson.

After graduation, he was a late-round draft choice of the Cleveland Browns. He never made the team and eventually took a job with State Farm Insurance. After two years with the company, he found his job uninspiring and tedious. It was at that time that he joined the Charleston Police Department and began his career in law enforcement.

Adam Stone demonstrated his own athletic prowess on the basketball court. While never attaining the level of recognition Marcus received, he did enjoy being a four-year starting point guard on Francis Marion University's basketball team. Although his college day were long gone, he continued to play ball in the highly competitive downtown Charleston league and with a group of his friends at a local gym on Saturday mornings. He was proud of the fact that he could still hold his own against the younger players.

~~~

The ceremony ended around 4:30 Friday afternoon. The crowd was dispersing when Marcus told Adam he needed to go home and see his wife, Makayla, before he returned to Lockwood. This was Adam and Marcus' Station Rotation weekend. Station Rotation was a program wherein each of the detective teams was required to cover the weekend night shifts every fifth week.

Adam also left and made the drive to Charleston Collegiate School on Johns Island to pick up his fourteen-year-old daughter, Piper. Adam had sold his James Island house several years ago and moved into a three-bedroom, two-bath apartment
~~~

with Piper. It had been over three years since his wife, Ann, had been brutally murdered at the hands of a serial killer. The murderer was eventually found and killed by Adam and several police officers. The third bedroom at the apartment was often used by Tracy Kendall, the mother of Adam's late wife. Since Ann's death, Tracy had become an even more integral part of their lives and would spend nights at the apartment with Piper when Adam was required to work late.

Piper, a superior student and an excellent soccer player, had practice after school until about 5:00. Adam pulled into the roundabout in front of the school's gym and waved to his daughter. It continued to amaze him how she'd grown. It seemed like only yesterday she was just a kid chasing the ball around in the back yard. But now she was on the brink of womanhood—showing a confidence and willingness to take on the challenges that lay ahead of her. His only regret was that Ann was not here to experience her metamorphosis.

"Hi, Dad," she said as she slid into Adam's Charger. "Can I go to the movies with Chloe tonight? Her mom said she'd drive."

"Sure, Sweetheart. Tracy will be staying at the apartment this weekend. I've got to be at the station. We can grab a bite to eat at home before I have to leave."

"That's cool," Piper said, "but you work too much, Dad."

Adam smiled and retorted, "Oh, you think so? Just wait until you graduate from college and get a job. Then we'll talk about working too much." Even though Adam dismissed Piper's comment, he often regretted the amount of time his job forced him to spend away from her.

Back in the apartment, Tracy had made soup and sandwiches. Adam barely had enough time to eat and take Max, their Lab mix and fourth member of the family, for a walk before he had to leave for the Lockwood station.

Marcus was already at his desk in the bullpen when Adam arrived. Early evenings on these weekend rotations were generally fairly quiet. Things normally picked up around 1:00 in the morning, but the patrol officers handled everything unless there was a shooting or some other event that required the attention of the detectives. Technology had come a long way in improving the efficiency and effectiveness of law enforcement. However, it had yet to replace an officer's cumbersome and time-consuming tradition of submitting paper reports. These weekend assignments were a good time for Adam and Marcus to catch up on their own paperwork.

As in most police stations, the coffee sucked, and Marcus left Lockwood about 10:00 p.m. to pick up coffee and muffins at the Coffee Cup. As soon as he returned, he passed a latte and muffin to Adam and said, "I need to talk to you about something."

Adam stopped in the middle of taking the top off the latte. "So, talk."

"All right. I'll get right to it. I've been thinking about leaving the force."

The comment obviously caught Adam off guard. He set down his coffee and was quiet for a moment before responding with a simple, "Why?"

"Makayla and I have been talking about it ever since I got hurt. Plus, her dad's restaurant supply business is doing really well, and he's been asking me to come aboard to help out for a while now."

A little over six months ago, Adam and Marcus were working a drug trafficking case when Marcus was attacked and brutally beaten by two men from the Sinaloa Cartel. He'd received a severe concussion, internal injuries, and multiple broken bones. It was touch and go for a time, but he eventually did recover. It took over a month of physical therapy before he was ready to rejoin the force—and even then, he continued to feel the effects of his injuries.

Adam had seen Marcus struggle after the attack, but the thought that he would ever consider leaving the department never crossed his mind. "I don't know what to say, brother. I know what you've been through since you got hurt, but this is in our blood, man. We bleed blue." Adam waved his arm around the bullpen. "This is what we do."

"I know," Marcus quickly replied. "I'll have my twenty-five in a few months and can leave with my full pension and benefits. I don't know how I'll handle life on the outside, but Makayla's been through a lot all these years." The life of a police officer's spouse is no walk in the park. The long and unpredictable hours and the dangerous world these officers live in often takes a toll on their marriage.

That comment about Makayla hit Adam hard. He could never quite convince himself that Ann's murder and its effect on Piper wasn't somehow related to his job. He was silent for some time until he finally said, "Marcus, you're my best friend and the best damn detective I know. If this is something you and Makayla need to do, I'm all in."

"I appreciate that. I just needed to get it off my chest. You need to know that it's something we're considering. Nothing's been finalized, and this thing may not even happen." Marcus smiled. "But either way, eat your muffin. We've got a long night ahead of us."

CHAPTER TWO

IT WAS QUIET for a Friday night in downtown Charleston. There were the normal traffic accidents, bar fights, and domestic incidents, but nothing requiring Adam and Marcus to leave the station until around 3:00 a.m.

A 911 call came into the Lockwood Communication Center at 3:02 Saturday morning from a woman who reported strange sounds and witnessed someone leaving her neighbor's house located at the corner of Rutledge and Queen across from Colonial Lake Park. After learning the subject residence was occupied by a Dr. Charles Richardson, officers arrived at the address a few minutes later. There had been no previous reports of any problems at the location, however, the officers approached without lights or siren and parked their patrol car several houses from the subject address. After identifying the woman who made the 911 call, they ordered her to remain inside her home and approached Richardson's house—their Glock 19's in the low ready position. They noticed the front door was partially ajar.

After situating themselves on either side of the door, they loudly announced their presence. "Police officers! Identify yourself! Identify yourself!"

There was no response, and the officer on the left gave his partner a hand signal indicating he would enter first. Using his left hand, he carefully eased the door open so they could see inside. It was dark, but there was enough ambient light to make out a body sprawled on the floor next to the entrance to the living room. He nodded to his partner and entered—his arms now extended in the front ready position. The living room was empty with the exception of a body of a man lying motionless on the floor. The other officer immediately followed him in and signaled he would clear the rest of the first floor. The first officer check the body for a pulse and found none. A short time later, his partner returned, and they proceeded upstairs. After confirming the second floor was also clear, they called headquarters. Not wanting to compromise the crime scene, the officers left and after checking the perimeter of the house, waited for the detectives to arrive.

Additional officers were dispatched, CSI personnel advised, and Adam and Marcus left for the crime scene. In the meantime, two additional squad cars showed up at the Rutledge residence, and officers were in the process of securing crime scene tape across the entrance when Adam and Marcus arrived on the scene. Most of the homes in the area were built in the early 1900s. Despite their age, they were well preserved, and there was no doubt that the area around Colonial Lake was upscale. The house where the body was found was on the smaller side but still valued well in excess of $1 million.

Adam approached the officers. "What have we got?"

"One adult male on the first floor. Deceased. Multiple gunshot wounds to chest and head. Inside clear and perimeter secured. EMS and CSI have been notified and are en route."

"Where is the individual who called it in?" Adam asked.

The officer pointed next door. "She's inside, sir. My partner is with her."

By now, lights were beginning to appear in several houses in the area and curious residents could be seen on their porches. "We're going next door," Adam said. "Make sure you keep the area clear."

They entered the woman's house and introduced themselves. Her name was Emma Harris. She was small, not much more than five foot, and appeared to be in her mid-to-late-seventies. She was holding a small white dog.

"Ma'am," Marcus began, "please tell us what you heard and saw before you called 911."

"Well now, Lady here gets me up most every night. Poor girl's getting old like me, and I have to take her out to pee, or she makes a mess. I don't mind getting up, though. At my age, I don't sleep very well anyway. Oh, dear, I remember when I could sleep like a baby. Anyway, I was outside, and Lady was doing her business when I heard something next door."

"That would be Dr. Richardson's house?" Marcus asked.

"Yes. Charles is his first name. But he doesn't like anyone calling him Charlie. Oh my, I hope Charles is all right."

"Can you describe the sound you heard?"

"Well, it was a funny sound—kind of like two 'snaps.' Then a second or two later there was another one. At first, I thought it might be that newspaper boy. He always throws the newspaper on our porches. But, Lord, it was the middle of the night. Then I saw a man leave Charles' house. He looked at me, and I think I surprised him. Then he jogged around the other side of the house. Can I get you something to drink? I can make some tea."

"No thank you, ma'am," Marcus said. "Will you please show us where you were when you heard those sounds and saw the person jogging around Dr. Richardson's house? You said it was a man, correct?"

"I think so. He had on one of those hooded sweatshirts. You know, the kind people wear in winter when it's cold."

"I see."

Ms. Harris took Adam and Marcus outside and down her front porch onto a small front lawn—positioning herself approximately five feet to the right of the bottom of the porch stairs.

"Thank you, ma'am. Now, could you describe the man?"

"Oh, dear. It was so dark. I just don't know."

"Could you tell if the person was tall or short, black or white?"

"I'm sorry, officer. I think he might have been white, but I only saw him for a second before he disappeared around the house. That's when I called 911. The lady that answered was very nice. I was a little nervous, but she calmed me down."

"Does Dr. Richardson live by himself?" Adam asked.

"Oh, yes. Sometimes he has lady friends over, but I know he lives there by himself. He rents the house from Dr. White. The Whites live on Daniel Island. They're very nice people."

"Thank you, Ms. Harris," Marcus said. "Just one more thing. Do you happen to know if Dr. Richardson has any relatives in the area?"

"Let me see. I do remember he told me he had a brother that lived in Pittsburgh, but he never mentioned any family here in Charleston."

"Thank you, Ms. Harris," Marcus said. "You've been very helpful. The officer will stay with you, and someone will be by shortly to take your statement."

After leaving Mrs. Harris, Adam commented, "I noticed she described the shots as being 'snaps.' Sounds like the gun probably had a suppressor which leads me to believe this wasn't a robbery. Sounds like it might have been a professional hit—but the question is why. The officer said the victim was shot several times to the chest and head. I figure the first two shots took him down, and the third was the kill shot to the head."

"Possibly," Marcus said. Adam and Marcus slipped on crime scene gloves and booties before entering. One tech was taking pictures of the body, and the other two were in the living room assessing the situation. Adam acknowledged the three techs and waited for the photographer to finish taking shots of the body.

Careful not to disturb anything, Marcus bent down to in-spect the body which was lying on its back. The dead man wore what looked like pajama bottoms and a blood-soaked Southern University T-shirt. He could see two wounds to the front of the man—one to the upper chest and one to the abdomen. The third bullet had entered the right frontal lobe directly above the eye socket. It was clear that was the fatal shot. He stood and scanned the living room. There was a large flat screen TV mounted above a granite fireplace. The hardwood floor was covered with several oriental rugs and the furniture was definitely high-end. Adam had checked out the kitchen and was now in the room to the right of the front door. It was a small office with two leather chairs and a good-sized wooden desk on which an Apple iMac® desktop computer sat.

When the two detectives continued their search upstairs, they found three bedrooms and two bathrooms. The largest room was the master bedroom, and another smaller bedroom was next to it. The third room was mirrored and filled with a variety of workout equipment and weights. The equipment looked to be new and high-tech.

Again, not wanting to disturb anything, they went down-stairs, left the house, and let the techs continue their work. As they were leaving, they saw that the blue and white coroner's van had arrived, and Alice O'Sullivan and her assistant were approaching the house. Alice was the Charleston County deputy coroner and had been around as long as Adam could remember.

O'Sullivan was wearing a Carolina Panthers' ball cap and dressed in a baggy sweatshirt and corduroy pants. "All right,

Stone. This better be good. I was asleep dreaming George Clooney was in my bedroom when I got the damn call."

Adam smiled and replied, "Sorry, Alice, but George is going to have to wait."

"Where's my customer?" she asked.

"The body's inside," Adam said. "The techs are still working the scene. Go on in and do what you do. We'll be around. Just let us know what you think when you're done."

Shortly after Alice left, one of Charleston's K-9 units stopped in front of the house, and an officer exited the vehicle along with a collared German Shepherd. Both Adam and Marcus knew the handler, Larry Miles, and his dog, Frodo, from several Special Operations drug task force investigations they'd worked together.

"Good morning, detectives," Miles said.

"How've you been, Larry?" Adam asked.

"Can't complain. Where are you on the investigation?"

Adam told Miles that O'Sullivan and CSI were still working the crime scene and explained what they'd learned so far about the murder. Fifteen minutes later, O'Sullivan exited the house followed by her assistant wheeling out the bagged corpse on a gurney. He put the body into the back of the van.

Marcus asked Alice what she'd discovered.

"The tech guys couldn't find any shell casings, so it looks like a revolver was used. Maybe a Ruger or a small S&W. The victim was shot three times, but CSI only recovered one slug. It looked like it could be a .22LR caliber, but ballistics can confirm that. I figure the other two are still inside the body. I'll verify that when I do the autopsy. Ballistics can give us a better indication of the murder weapon."

"When do you think you'll get started on the autopsy?" Marcus asked.

"I need to sleep a little more, but I'll get on it as soon as I get up. Hopefully, I'll have some preliminaries for you sometime later today. Good luck on your investigation, boys. I'm out of here. George is waiting for me."

Adam went inside to check with the techs. He returned a moment later and gave the go ahead for Frodo to do his thing.

Once inside the house, Miles unclipped the dog's leash, and he began probing the living room for narcotics. Frodo was all business as he systematically moved through each section of the room searching for the familiar scent of drugs. Adam continued to be amazed at what these dogs could do. Narcotic detection dogs, or "sniffers" as they are called, are trained to recognize seven basic odors which allows them to detect narcotics of different types and compositions. He'd heard that some scientists believe these trained sniffers' sense of smell is tens of thousands of times more sensitive than what a human is capable of smelling. And the unique anatomy of a dog's nose allows a K-9 to detect odors at concentrations of 1 to 2 parts per trillion—that right, trillion!

Frodo finished sweeping the first floor and eventually moved upstairs to the master bedroom. He was working the bedroom when he suddenly stopped and sat directly in front of one of the closets. Miles moved the hanging clothes aside exposing a flat wooden panel painted the same color as the sheetrock. The panel measured approximately 3' by 4' and was held against the back wall by four corner screws. Marcus removed his multipurpose pocketknife and used the small Phillips-head attachment to remove the panel. There was a heavy-duty electronic safe that appeared to be bolted flush to the wall.

"Good boy, Frodo!" Miles praised his dog. "That's my good boy! Well, detectives, I think we might have just hit the jackpot. There's definitely drugs inside there. That's one of those fingerprint safes. You're going to need a professional to open that sucker."

Marcus took a few pictures of the wooden panel and safe while Adam called headquarters requesting a locksmith.

When Marcus finished taking pictures, he retrieved the keys to Richardson's BMW 530i from one of the techs and had Frodo check out the car. The dog sniffed around the exterior, interior, and the trunk area of the BMW, but no drugs were found. Adam and Marcus thanked Miles, and he told them he'd get his report to them later that day. The BMW would be transferred to the forensic garage at Lockwood where it would be disassembled and thoroughly searched.

After Miles left, Adam told Marcus that headquarters had gotten ahold of their locksmith, and he'd be here in about a half-hour. "Come on, buddy, let's take another look inside."

They entered the house and went directly to the small first-floor office just to the right of the entrance. CSI had taken Richardson's Apple iMac®, and the computer techs at Lockwood would analyze its contents. Adam began going through the center desk drawer and found a box of Richardson's business cards. The cards identified Dr. Charles Richardson as president of PRO Care Physical Therapy and listed its address as 2116 Remount Road in North Charleston. There was a stack of business cards held together by a rubber band. Adam removed it and went through the cards. Nothing jumped out at him, but they would need to follow up on these contacts later. Richardson's personal checkbook was also in the center drawer. Adam flipped through it and noticed the balance was maintained at around $5,000 but found nothing overly suspicious.

There were several file folders in one of the larger side drawers. The folders contained receipts, car and health insurance agreements, and several other documents—none of which seemed to be anything out of the ordinary. Another drawer contained several brochures and catalogs for physical therapy products and equipment.

The desk had a glass top, and Adam noticed four business cards were slid under it. One of the cards listed a Susan Novak as an administrative assistant at PRO Care. The other business cards showed the names and addresses of three physicians in the Charleston area—Samuel Morgan, Nathan Bell, and Ronald Jefferson. Adam used his cell phone to take pictures of the four cards and copied their names and phone numbers in his notepad.

"Marcus, come here and take a look at this."

Marcus noted the fact that pain management was the specialty of all three of them. "It would make sense for a physical therapist like Richardson to receive referrals from those types of doctors. It also seems likely that Richardson may have referred his clients to a pain specialist."

"I hear you," Adam answered. "On the surface there doesn't seem to be anything terribly wrong with this picture. But look where Richardson lives. This house is definitely in the high-rent district. I bet he pays around $4,000 or $5,000 for rent each month, he drives a new $60,000 BMW, and look at the way his place is furnished. Those oriental rugs and original art must cost more than I make in a year. I don't know how much a physical therapist makes, but it's sure as hell nowhere near enough to pay for this kind of lifestyle."

"You're right," Marcus replied. "And did you see the clothes in his closet? I wouldn't be surprised if those suits cost $3,000 or $4,000. Maybe mommy and daddy left him an inheritance, but whatever the case, Richardson had to have another source of money to live like this. We need to find out what's in his safe and check out his business, but something about this whole scene doesn't smell right."

They spent the next twenty-five minutes checking the rest of the house for any clues that would shed more light on what might have happened to Charles Richardson. Nothing of substance was found.

The Lowcountry Lock & Safe van pulled up, and a tall, thin man got out carrying a case about the size of a standard piece of luggage. "Hello, detectives. Name's Burt Willis. I got the call from Lockwood."

Adam and Marcus introduced themselves, and on the way into the house, Marcus explained the police dog's discovery in the upstairs bedroom closet. "I don't know anything about safes, but this one looks pretty substantial."

Once in the upstairs bedroom, Willis set his case aside and bent down into a catcher's stance to study the safe. "That's a Barska Biometric safe. It's programed to be accessed by using the owner's fingerprint. I'm going to have to drill this one."

"Go ahead and do whatever you need to do," Adam said.

"All right. This is going to take about thirty minutes." Willis had Adam sign a waiver and then opened his case and removed a templet containing two sets of four small square openings on either side of a center point. He placed the center point of the templet over the point at which he would drill out the locking mechanism and marked each hole. After drilling the eight marked holes, he removed a piece of bracketed metal that would be used to precisely center the drill in the proper location. Once centered, it was secured to the safe with eight self-setting bolts. The electric power drill with a long titanium drill bit was secured to the bracket. He put on gloves and safety goggles and began drilling. It was an exceedingly slow process with Willis constantly adjusting the drill and cooling the drill bit. When the drilling was finally completed, Willis removed his goggles and opened the door of the safe.

"Well, I'll be damned," Marcus muttered. He took out his cell phone and took a picture of what was inside the safe.

The upper portion was filled with large plastic bottles—each containing oxycodone pills. Adam put on crime scene gloves and removed one of the bottles. The label read *oxicodona*—the Spanish spelling of oxycodone and indicated that the bottle held two thousand 30 mg pills. There were also several rubber-banded stacks of $50 and $100 bills. The lower section of the safe held three passports, a flash drive, and six burner phones. On closer inspection, Adam found a key with the number 128 attached to it.

He removed the key. "I wonder what this is to?"

"Good luck with that," Marcus answered. "Could be almost anything."

Adam then removed one of the stacks of bills and pointed to the safe. "Looks like our physical therapist was dealing a different kind of therapy on the side."

Marcus shook his head and said, "If he's dealing this much OXY, there's no way he's not connected."

"Agreed," Adam said. "There must be at least fifty thousand pills in there, and you got to figure those three doctors whose cards were on Richardson's desk are probably in on this. We know South Carolina doctors can fill their own prescriptions of controlled substances out of their office. Technically, they're limited to 30 pills per prescription, but it's up to the doctor to report the number and amount of the prescriptions they fill. It's no secret there's plenty of doctors out there who run pill mills and only report what they need to in order to stay under the radar. There's also a limit to what docs can charge for these drugs. But, again, you got to figure these doctors know which of their patients are willing to pay a hell of a lot more. These asshole doctors are no better than street pushers."

Marcus told Burt Willis to keep what he just saw to himself. "The longer we can keep what we found quiet, the better chance we've got solving this thing."

"Hey, guys," he answered, "my lips are sealed. Your police department is one of my biggest customers. No way am I going to mess that up."

"Good," Marcus said. "You need to write out some notes to yourself about what you did here. There's a chance you might need to testify if this thing makes it to a trial. You did a good job, Willis. Now, get yourself packed up and out of here."

"Yes, sir!"

After Willis left, Marcus told the forensic techs the items in the safe needed to be bagged, sealed, and identified. It was absolutely critical that the chain of custody be maintained to guarantee the integrity of the evidence collected and processed. If anyone handle evidence in an unsecured or sloppy manner, it was said they "*pulled an O.J.*" The phrase obviously referring to the O.J. Simpson trial.

~~~

It was early Sunday morning, and night was giving way to the gray light of dawn. Adam told the patrol officers to stay at the scene until forensics finished up and to make sure the house was locked up and the front door taped. He instructed them to talk to the neighbors to see if they'd witnessed anything and canvass the area around the lake for anything that might be linked to the murder.
~~~

Adam and Marcus were driving back to the station when Adam said, "Listen, when we get back, I'll get the murder book started, and you can catch a few hours of sleep. I'll get some shuteye when you get up. I figure the computer guys will have something for us off Richardson's computer and cell phone early this afternoon. And, hopefully, Alice will have some preliminaries from the autopsy by later today."

"Works for me," Marcus answered. "Makayla will be pissed, but she understands. We'll also need to find a phone number for Richardson's brother in Pittsburgh and let him know what happen. We can interview him later."

"I'm sure there's a key for Richardson's office on the key chain the techs recovered from his house. If we can get Judge Roberts to sign off on a warrant by late afternoon, we can use it to check out Richardson's office this evening."

"Wait," Marcus said, "that reminds me. We need to bring Boyer up to speed on what we have. I'm sure he knows about the murder by now. We can also ask him to check with our undercover street people to see what they know about the distribution of opioids around here. I remember four or five years ago when a Jersey mob-connected guy by the name of Max DiMarco was running a scheme to steal narcotics from Mercy Hospital. An ex-cop who ran a police dog training business out in Johns Island and his buddies took down DiMarco and a few of his thugs out in a North Charleston warehouse."

"I remember that," Adam recalled. "We know the Posse, the Bloods, and the cartel were never that interested in pills. They stuck with the hard stuff. It was the local mob that had connections to Jersey and Chicago that ran the distribution of opioids. The Scorpions and a few other biker gangs are in the methamphetamine business around here, but it's not really organized. It's my guess that if Richardson is connected, it's going to be with Nick Santoro. Remember Nick's the nephew of Eddie Santoro who runs the mafia's business on the South Side of Chicago."

"All that may be so but don't forget Santoro is a prime suspect in Joe Wallace and Tanya Scarcella's murders."

Adam shook his head. "Nick Santoro is always a suspect in something, and it's never stopped him from doing the mob's business."

By this time, they were back at the station, and Marcus headed to a room on the second floor called the Bunkhouse to sleep for a few hours. Adam settled in at his desk to start on the murder book. The Richardson murder was fresh, and they both knew there'd be little rest for the next several days.

ABOUT THE AUTHOR

Geoff Collins holds graduate degrees in business and finance and a master's degree in education. He has held multiple management positions in Fortune 500 companies and was CEO of a Midwest advertising and public relations firm.

After a successful career in business, he taught elementary school for fifteen years. His passion for teaching reading and writing to his students led to a career as an author of both children stories and adult mysteries.

Geoff lives on Johns Island, South Carolina, with his wife, Sally. He has three grown children, Max, Leigh, and KC, and four grandchildren, John, Collin, Cora, and Lily.

OTHER BOOKS BY
GEOFF AND ART COLLINS

NIKKI AND THE TREE KEEPER

"What a wonderful and lovely tale!"

"Nikki is a heart-warming and inspirational story of finding your place in the world."

"Nikki and the Tree Keeper is magical."

"The illustrations are beautiful and add so much to the book."

www.booksbycollins.com

THE CHRISTMAS TOKEN

"The Christmas Token is a heart-warming holiday tale about generosity, memories, and family."

"The artwork in this tender story is superior!"

"The Christmas Token should become a family tradition to read as the Christmas season begins!"

"Excellent!"

"Lovely book! My kids have read it many times over the holidays."

www.booksbycollins.com

THE ADVENTURES OF ARCHIBALD & JOCKABEB

"One of a kind!"

This is the best book EVER!!!!!! Dragons, Indians, horses, evil crows, there is nothing like it! I loved it ... can't wait for more adventures to come.

"A majestic tale—*Harry Potter* meets *The Indian in the Cupboard*"

Loved reading these books. I quickly got hooked, dug in, and engaged with the characters. Wonderful stories.

"Rich in vocabulary!"

This book is rich in vocabulary. I can't wait to read all the other Archibald and Jockabeb books!

"Best of the best!"

In the Forest is an outstanding book! The characters are great and help make the wonderful story come together.

"Terrific series of action books!"

www.booksbycollins.com

WHITE CLOUD AND THE GOLDEN CANYON

Excellent Native American tale for children and adults alike.

Wonderful life lessons for all.

Very enjoyable and true to our culture. (Akta Lakota Museum)

www.booksbycollins.com

THE BLACK CREEK MYSTERIES

Alex Foster and Travis Sanders live in a small southern Ohio farm town named Rivers Edge. Their first adventure takes them to the remote desert town of Sunshine, Arizona, where they find themselves in the middle of the Legend of the Apache Death Cave. The following summer, after Alex and Travis graduate from high school, they head to the small fishing town of Black Creek, Maine, for a relaxing vacation before they both head off to college. Their trip becomes anything but relaxing when they discover a mysterious creature in an underwater cave and a network of deadly gunrunners.

www.booksbycollins.com

THE MERCY KILLINGS

"Well Written … Interesting Characters and Plenty of Suspense"

Good mystery with interesting characters and plenty of suspense. A cybersecurity expert is hired to determine if narcotics theft is taking place at Charleston SC hospital and who is behind it. Well written with lots of fascinating details.

"Wonderfully Crafted Story Set in Charleston"

Wonderfully crafted story set in Charleston, SC—great story line and vivid imagery. Collins follows Giordano with insight and honesty. Can't wait for Nick's next adventure.

"A Fast and Exciting Read"

The book was a fast read. It was exciting and held my interest throughout. Hope to see more from this author.

www.booksbycollins.com

THE TOOLS OF THE TRADE

Mario Rossini's Jersey syndicate, the Beltran-Lyve Cartel, and the KKK's Confederate White Knights are all battling for control over Charleston's drug trade. Nick Giordano and his friends once again find themselves entangled in the fight. And this time they may all be targets for the legendary Mafia hitman, Carlos Tucci.

"Another Wild Ride"

Tools of the Trade takes us on another wild ride with Nick Giordano and his crew. Collins, as he did with his previous book in this three-part series (volume three is coming in 2019), deftly weaves on intricate story line that builds to a satisfying, thrilling end. Highly recommend Collins, a writer who deserves a vast readership.

"Excitement and Suspense"

Excitement and suspense as mafia and white supremacists fight over the drug market in Charleston SC. Characters well-developed and interesting story line.

www.booksbycollins.com

SHARK BAIT

Nick Giordano and his friends are drawn into the dark and dangerous world of the Russian mafia. The East Coast Russian mafia boss, Dimitri "The Shark" Pavlov, and his enforcer, Viktor Dudko, are using Charleston's Port Authority terminals for drug smuggling and human trafficking.

"Hopefully More to Come"

In this series, which sadly wraps here with Book Three, Collins found a higher gear with each, serving up a fresh batch of nasty folks for the series' core characters to root out and take down. That the books were set in Charleston only added to their delight. The only rotten aspect here is that this is the last we'll see of Nick Giordano and his pals—that is, unless, this crew comes around for cameos in one of Collins' future works. Hats off!

www.booksbycollins.com

A DEATH IN THE FAMILY

Detective Adam Stone and his partner, Marcus Williams, are part of Charleston's elite Organized Crime Unit investigating a spike in the city's heroin and fentanyl drug trade. During a raid of a major drug distribution house, the shot-caller of the Bloods is shot and killed by Adam. Shortly after that, his wife, Ann, is found murdered. Initially, the Bloods are the obvious suspects. However, as the story unfolds, several other women are murdered, and the list of possible suspects grows. It soon becomes apparent that there is a serial killer roaming the street of Charleston.

www.booksbycollins.com

                    Geoff Collins

Reading Partners is a nonprofit literacy organization that recruits and trains community volunteers to provide one-on-one reading tutoring to students in under-resourced schools across the country. This highly effective program has helped thousands of children master the fundamental reading skills they need to succeed in school and beyond. For more information, please visit www.readingpartners.org.

"Literacy is not a luxury; it is a right and a responsibility. If our world is to meet the challenges of the twenty-first century we must harness the energy and creativity of all our citizens."

–President Bill Clinton

www.ingramcontent.com/pod-product-compliance
Lightning Source LLC
Chambersburg PA
CBHW050515190726
48284CB00003B/811